Crunch

Also by
LESLIE CONNOR

Waiting for Normal

LESLIE CONNOR

Crunch

KATHERINE TEGEN BOOKS
An Imprint of HarperCollins Publishers

Katherine Tegen Books
is an imprint of HarperCollins Publishers.

www.harpercollinschildrens.com

Library of Congress Cataloging-in-Publication Data
Connor, Leslie.
  Crunch / Leslie Connor. — 1st ed.
    p.   cm.
Summary: Fourteen-year-old Dewey Marriss juggles the management of the
family's bicycle repair business while sharing the household and farm duties with
his siblings when a sudden energy crisis leaves their parents stranded far from
home.
  ISBN 978-0-06-169229-1 (trade bdg.)
  ISBN 978-0-06-169233-8 (lib. bdg.)
  [1. Self-reliance—Fiction. 2. Coming of age—Fiction. 3. Brothers and sisters—
Fiction. 4. Family problems—Fiction. 5. Bicycles and bicycling—Fiction.
6. Business enterprises—Fiction. 7. Energy conservation—Fiction.] I. Title.
PZ7.C76442 Cr 2010   2009024339
[Fic]—dc22   CIP
                                                                          AC

Typography by Andrea Vandergrift
10 11 12 13 14   LP/RRDB   10 9 8 7 6 5 4 3 2 1

First Edition

For Jonathan, my tandem partner
(Yes! I'm pedaling!)

1

I SAW IT LIKE THIS: A SINGLE WORKER AT SOME faraway oil refinery with his head tilted down, peering into a pipe, waiting for one more drop that never came. Doesn't mean it was really like that. It probably wasn't. But that's what I saw in my mind's eye the night our parents called to say that their trip had been extended. Indefinitely.

It was a five-sibling footrace for the phone, and I won.

"Dad? Dad, is that you?" I waited and listened.

"Sure is, Dewey. Can you hear me all right?"

"Pretty well," I said. But the signal wasn't great, and my pulse was thumping in my ears.

My older sister, Lil, pushed close to me. We

shared the receiver.

"Everyone doing okay?" Dad asked.

"We're all right," I said.

"And how about the *situation*?" he asked. "What's the view from the home front?"

"Red flags are up at every fuel pump for miles," I said. I lost my breath on the words. "No gas. No diesel. They say it's the same everywhere. Is that true, Dad? There's no fuel?"

His answer came slowly. "It appears to be so," he said. "Pumps are dry clear across the country."

Lil leaned away from the phone and whispered, "Shoot!" We both knew what was coming next.

"I'm just so sorry," Dad said. "Mom and I are still caught up here practically in Canada. I've got a stack of ration cards, but at the moment, they're not worth a roll of toilet tissue."

I tried to give him a laugh, but nothing came out. Dad will joke even in tough situations. But he was sincere about that apology. They had thought twice about having Mom go. But this was the anniversary trip. Number *twenty*. None of us had wanted them to miss it.

2

Dad's main job is making deliveries all up and down the coast of New England. He drives an eighteen-foot box truck with a roll-up rear door. He can maneuver it in and out of all the nooks and crannies in the seashore towns. He's an independent—makes up his own route and schedule. Each July Mom rides with him for a few days to celebrate their wedding anniversary. It's not a fancy trip. I sometimes think of it as the Week That Mom Goes to Work with Dad. But Mom loves the scenery, and she says that it's only right that she support Dad in his lifelong search for the best basket of fish-and-chips in New England.

It used to be they'd get someone to stay with us kids. But this year, Lil was eighteen, I was fourteen, and Vince was thirteen. Angus and Eva, our twins, were only five. But to Mom that meant they were no longer babies. With all of us Marriss kids being the *embodiment of responsibility* (Lil came up with that one), it was decided that we could manage on our own. And we could. And we were. So far.

"What's the news from the Bike Barn, Dewey?" Dad asked.

"It's busy," I said.

Okay. Not exactly *news*. The Marriss Bike Barn had been humming all summer. We do repairs. Hard times at the gas pumps had meant good times for the bike biz. People were relying on pedal power—big-time. If there was news, it was that we were busier now than Dad had ever seen it. But I couldn't quite bring myself to tell him that.

"Vince and I have it covered," I said. My brother faked a cheery smile, then let his face collapse into a gory frown. I couldn't blame him. I was the one who'd talked Dad into letting me run the shop while he and Mom were away. And I was the one who'd roped Vince into it with me.

"Dew, just be careful you don't get overwhelmed," Dad said.

I didn't say anything. There was a pause on the line. Lil pressed closer to me—practically climbing up my ankles. I shuffled sideways.

Dad went on. "Now, Lil's class starts tomorrow. She should still go. That's paramount. No reason you guys can't make that work, especially with Angus and Eva in Sea Camp all morning."

Lil turned away again. This time, she fired a euphoric "Yesss!" toward the ceiling.

"I'm afraid we're not going to get an overnight solution to this fuel thing," Dad said. "But mark my words, life will move on. You'll see it. And if something doesn't break within a few days, I suppose we'll try to get Mom down to a train. Somehow. Not sure how we'll get her out of the hinterlands . . ." Now he was thinking out loud. "I'll have to stay with the truck. I guess we're in a game of wait and see."

Lil took the phone from me with a twist of her wrist. "Dad, don't sweat this," she said. "I'll only be in class until one o'clock. Then I'm home. Mom should stay with you. Besides, how long can it go on? And Dad, how long have I been doing this?"

She meant how long had she been taking care of younger kids. The answer: a long time. She was already thirteen by the time Angus and Eva were born. (I think those two just figure they have two moms.)

Our parents gave Lil some instructions and fired off the reminder that they expected us all to take care of one another. I heard that loud and clear from my place beside Lil's shoulder. After they hung up, the five of us stood in the kitchen for several seconds without saying anything. Lil and Vince and I knew we'd have to somehow play it happy for Angus and Eva. This wasn't fun news for anybody, but try telling a pair of five-year-olds that you don't know when their mommy and daddy are coming home.

"I-I just really wanted them to come home *now*," Angus said. He blinked back tears.

"W-well, how many more days?" Eva wanted to know. She was trying hard to suck it up too.

Lil squatted down, arms wide. "Okay, come here," she said. She gathered them in. "I know you miss them. But you have Vince and Dew and me. We're going to keep on taking good care of you. And when there is enough fuel again, Mom and Dad will come straight home to us. This is just some bad luck. Nobody could have known."

But part of me was thinking that we *should*

have known. Or somebody should have. Fuel reserves had been low all winter and they'd stayed that way through the spring. The news had been full of stories—everything from people giving up their gas guzzlers and lawn mowers to high prices and ration cards. There had been long lists of all the goods and services that were slowed because of the fuel shortage.

But now, in this second week in a hot July, suddenly *shortage* wasn't the right word anymore. Shortage would mean there wasn't *enough*. Instead, there wasn't *any*.

Vince hit the nail on the head. (He usually does.)

"This," he said, "is a *crunch*."

2

EARLY THE NEXT MORNING, LIL JAMMED A BOX
of drawing charcoal and two sketchbooks in her
backpack, which was already stuffed with art
supplies. Angus and Eva looked on. They were a
little bleary and not so happy to see Lil—the next
best thing to Mom—pack up and leave. We'd distracted them enough to avoid major meltdowns—
at least so far. (Lil had allowed double desserts
and late bedtimes, and I think she'd slept in their
room.) But Angus and Eva did keep asking, "So
now *when* will Mom and Dad come home? *When*
can they get the tank filled up?" We couldn't
supply the answer, and Lil didn't try. She stuck to
telling them what she *did* know.

"Today's really nothing new. You guys will be

at Sea Camp again. *Just like last week.* Dewey will take you. Vince will pick you up. *Just like . . .*" She waited.

". . . *last week,*" Angus said.

"Right. And everything else today will be *just like yesterday.* Except that I'm going to Elm City for the morning."

"All week long," I added.

"R-right," Lil said. She gave me an eye roll to let me know I wasn't helping. She focused on the twins again. "What I mean is, we all know what we are doing. And we all have chores. *Just like yesterday.* Angus and Eva, you will take care of the henhouse. *Just like . . .*"

". . . *yesterday,*" Angus finished, and he managed a tiny smile.

Vince tuned up. "And I will milk our goats. And I will pasteurize our goats' milk. Then I will be a slave in our bike shop." He pressed the words at me. "*Just. Like. Yesterday.*"

Lil snorted a laugh. Then she just cracked up.

Who's not helping now? I thought. Truth was, Vince liked working on bikes. Just not as much as

I did. The killer: He was a better mechanic than I was. There was just one thing he couldn't stand about the Bike Barn, and that was dealing with people. I hadn't said so out loud, but after five full days of running the shop on our own, well, I'll just say that both Vince and I had been ready for Dad to come home.

Lil hugged Angus and Eva, then she bumped knuckles with Vince and me. She hoisted about ninety-seven pounds of art supplies onto her back and headed out on foot to catch the 7:16 Shore-Liner into Elm City. "You're leaving early," I called after her.

"Yeah, well, can you imagine what the trains will be like today?" she said. She shifted the load on her back.

"Why don't you bike to the station?" I called after her. It wasn't a long walk, but she was teetering under the weight of that pack.

"Too many thefts from the racks at the depot. I'm not risking it." She waved an arm over her head and started out.

I realized something. She had *totally* lied. Today

was not just like yesterday—not for Lil. An art class at Elm City College was completely new. She had worked hard to win this scholarship. She was top pick for a two-week session called Innovative Art Themes Intensive. (Too many words if you ask me, but the *intense* part came through loud and clear.) Talk about looking forward to something.

"Hey, Lil!" I hollered. "Good luck!"

She called back to me. "Thank you, Dew!"

I brought my hands together in a loud clap and took my new post. When the oldest is away, the second oldest takes command. Being the parents, Lil calls it, and it's automatic. Of course, nobody takes charge quite like Lil does, but I have my own way of dealing with little siblings. Even sad ones.

I turned to Angus and Eva, made monster claws, and growled, "What are *you* doin' still standing here? Do you *want* to be *late* for *Sea Camp*? RA-ARRrrrrr!"

They giggled madly.

"Go get those eggs!" I shooed them toward the coop.

Two red hens hurried behind the twins. We

called them the Athletes because they flapped up over the fence of the turnout every day to range free.

Vince came swinging by with his milk buckets and gave me a loud yawn in the face. Our dogs, shaggy old Goodness and sleek young Greatness, trotted beside him.

"Hey, think the Bike Barn will be busy today?" I asked.

As he passed me he nodded and said, "Just. Like. Yesterday."

3

WE LIVE ON THE HIGHWAY. WELL, OUR ADDRESS is Bridle Path Lane. Maybe it was a bridle path a hundred years ago, but things change. Now it's the on-ramp at exit 60. (Dad calls it a short commute to work.) Sounds like a cruddy place to live, but it's not. Our driveway takes us back behind the trees about a hundred yards, then opens onto the farmhouse, barns, and pasture. Lil says, "Heard of secret gardens? We're a 'secret farm.'" Mostly we just grow food for ourselves. But over the years, people have discovered our fresh eggs and goat's milk. This summer, they'd been coming for the Bike Barn.

We'd always been a tiny business. Just something for Dad to do between hauls. It used to be days between new customers—sometimes longer. Our "cash register" was just a peppermint tin. But suddenly bikes were more important. There I was, checking in my third new customer of the morning and trying to make sure Angus and Eva were ready for Sea Camp all at the same time.

Customers had been coming in clusters, either early or late in the day. We didn't keep official hours. Something to talk to Dad about, I thought. Vince wheeled a finished job past me to the front of the shop. Then he slinked back out to the paddock to hide.

"It's McKinnon," the woman told me. "Big M, small c, big K—" She began to spell, which always confused me. I wrote quickly, trying to keep up. "Now, look, I have a toddler." She shifted a baby from one hip to the other. "This bike is how we get around right now, and that includes getting to work." (It was a familiar story.) "So I need it back as soon as possible." She leaned forward. "When will that be?"

In the past five days I had learned to stick to facts. "Well, we do repairs in the order that they come in," I said. "Unless we have to wait for the parts. But I think this cable is your only problem." I squeezed the floppy brake lever.

"Um, excuse me," Eva whispered at my side. She swung her bike helmet against my knee a few times as she spoke. "Dewey, aren't we going to be late?"

"I'm almost done, Eva. Put your helmet on and get Angus," I said.

"So, the cable," Mrs. McKinnon said. "You have it?"

"Yes. But we also have a lot of repairs ahead of you." I stepped aside to let her glimpse the bikes beneath the overhang in the paddock.

"Oh yuck," she said. She and her toddler seemed to wilt together. "So, any chance it'll be tomorrow? The next day?"

"I can't promise," I said. "But we will call you as soon as it's ready."

"Okay," she said with a sigh. "Oh, and I heard you have goat's milk? We're allergic and Shoreland's Market didn't get their delivery." She sighed and added, "Then again, who did?"

"Milk and eggs are in the small fridge on the porch." I pointed toward the house. "It's self-serve. Make your own change from the teapot. Please return the empties."

"Okay. And can we pat the goats while we're here?"

"You can!" Eva chimed. "They're sweeties. We have Willa and Camilla, Petunia and Mayhem—"

"Eva, I asked you to find Angus," I said. She gave me a frown. I could have cracked her up with a growl or a roar but not in front of a customer. "The goats love attention," I explained. "But they'll chew your clothes and eat your hair, so be careful. And skip the farthest pasture. That's our billy goat, and he's smelly. You don't want to pat him."

"His name is Sprocket," Eva said. "He butted me in the butt once."

Our customer smiled for the first time. "This is like being on a field trip," she said, and she watched the Athletes strut by.

Mrs. McKinnon and her baby headed toward the pasture. I wheeled her bike through the shop, mumbling, "Always something to do at the Secret Farm," then I called, "Okay, Vince. Come out, come out, wherever you are. I'm taking the twins. Be back as fast as I can." Then I called, "Angus! Eva!" They appeared. I made monster claws. "Let's *r-r-ride*!" I growled.

4

I'VE GOT CRAZY-GOOD HEARING. ALL I HAVE TO do is run a little sound check to know whether there's a lot of traffic on the highway. This morning, I couldn't pick up a single singing tire. No whistling eighteen-wheelers. Not a hum. Not a whoosh.

I was dying to go have a look at the interstate, but it made no sense to take the twins out to the ramp. We'd worn a good shortcut between the yards, and that was the best way to get on the road to town and the beaches. Well, best way, except for one thing: our neighbor, Mr. Spivey. His yard backs up to ours. They say good fences make good neighbors. I say our fence will never be good enough.

We always tried to avoid him, though it wasn't

easy. I leaned over my handlebars and in a low voice I coaxed Angus and Eva. "Pedal, pedal," I said, and they did. But Mr. Spivey's head popped up like he had radar anyway.

"Darn," I whispered. I just didn't want to deal with him. He followed us with a squinty stare, so I called out, "Good morning!" Dad had always said, "Offer a greeting. Maintain a neighborly stance even if he doesn't return the enthusiasm."

Believe me, he *never* did. He was more likely to start giving us what for about something. Anything. The bike path barely grazes his property, yet he had a way of making us feel like we were trespassing. But if ever there was a trespasser in our neighborhood, it was the Spive himself. In fact, trespassing was his daily habit.

Earlier that morning, Angus and Eva had given me the egg report.

"We got nineteen eggs," Angus had said.

"Yeah, but really twenty-one," Eva had added as she'd set them into cartons.

"Was Mr. Spivey in the coop?" I'd asked.

"Yep. He took two," Angus had said.

"But he pretended that he didn't. He always pretends that." Eva had shrugged. Then she'd smiled. "He just put them in his shirt. Again."

"Yeah, the snake . . ." I had said. But I'd stopped because it was important to Mom and Dad that none of us mess with what Mom called "the beautiful matter-of-factness" with which our twins viewed our neighbor. The rest of us marveled at his lack of shame. It didn't help that the Spive had a sort of bend-and-scurry way of walking that made him look, well, just like a thief.

It wasn't just eggs. It was kindling wood and raspberries, a zucchini here and some sugar snap peas there. All just a little at a time. Vince once said, "What's his is his, and what's ours is his too." Dad had laughed and said, "Right! But what's a couple of eggs between neighbors?"

Whatever. We got past him today without a scolding. A triumph.

The twins and I turned off the path onto the empty road to town. I was pedaling in a ridiculously high gear. Spinning. Three miles to go. Angus and Eva were good riders. But little bikes only roll so fast, and five-year-olds can provide only so much power. And Angus had to dodge every pinecone and maple wing along the way.

"Those are going to be trees," he insisted. "And I like trees." He swerved and hollered, "Acorn!"

I accidentally flattened it under my tire and whispered, "Oops."

I would not normally have cared about the *crawl* to Sea Camp. But there were all those repairs to get back to at the Bike Barn. Also, Vince was alone and the busier we got, the more uncomfortable it made him to be left with the shop. Still, Angus and Eva came first. They were mine alone to care for from home to camp. That was the plan. Something to stick to. My turn to be the parents.

"Stay to the right, guys," I called up to them. "Just in case." But all three of us knew no cars were coming. Boston Post Road had never been easier to cross.

We arrived at the screened pavilion at the town beach not *too* much later. "Excellent riding," I told them.

"You too, Dewey," said Eva.

I grinned and handed them their lunches from my handlebar bag. I wheeled the two junior bikes around to the shady side of the pavilion and hung the helmets over their handlebars. The twins went up to the porch and the door opened. Mattie greeted them and herded them inside. She waved to me.

"How's that bike tire?" I asked. I had replaced an inner tube for her just the day before.

"I'm rolling along again, thanks to you, Dewey!"

Mattie and I were old pals. I'd been a Sea Camper once, and so had Vince. Mattie lived up a narrow lane from the beach in a little cottage that her dad had winterized. Everyone called Mattie's dad Pop Chilly. Everybody in town knew him. He'd driven the ice-cream truck for years. This summer, gas prices had put him out of business.

"I really need that old bike right now," Mattie said.

"You and everyone else! We just keep checking 'em in at the shop," I said. "And the best part is giving them back."

"And how's it going?" Mattie asked.

"All right," I said. "A few tough jobs that might have to wait. Mom and Dad are stuck up near the border. No diesel," I added.

"Oh no!" Mattie wilted against the doorjamb. "That's right. You guys are home alone."

"Except there are five of us." I shrugged and smiled.

"True that," Mattie said. "Well . . . hey, what say we cook together tonight at your place? Pop and I took the boat out early this morning." She grinned. "We raked in a big bucket of littlenecks."

I groaned right out loud—in a good way. Nothing was better than Mattie's clam chowder.

"Are you sure?" I said. But before she could answer I added, "We've got everything else." I started to count it off on my fingers. "Milk, potatoes, onions. And I think there's one last quart of Mom's corn in the cellar still. Vince and I can get a pit fire going and—"

"Sounds perfect," Mattie said. "Pop will be pleased. You go get on with your day and we'll see you later." She waved good-bye.

I got back onto the road, pumped up some speed, and flew along the centerline on my way back up to the Boston Post Road. I flashed on the Fourth of July—*any* Fourth of July. That's what this felt like—that fifteen minutes before the parade when the cops have closed the road and the cyclists own it. Of course, Officer Runkle always owns it with us. Runks is our town bike cop. He's also a customer at the Bike Barn and a family friend.

I played my front tire against the double yellow line. I felt a sense of *something*—freedom or ownership. I liked it. But already I was thinking that I wasn't sure how long I wanted it to last.

5

I WAS BACK IN THE HOUSE LESS THAN THREE minutes when Lil called to say that her summer session at Elm City College had been flat-out canceled before the first day even got under way.

"It's this fuel thing, Dewey. It's insane!" Lil was steamed and talking nonstop. "They're saying no one can get here, so it's over. But *I* got here! How about a little *commitment*? And listen, there was a wicked crush at the train station. I couldn't even get on the Shore-Liner out of here."

"Well, what are you going to do?" I asked. I was trying to stay cool. I like to know the plan and stick to it. But it seemed to me a lot of Marriss family plans were unraveling.

"I'm going to walk," said Lil.

"Walk? Lil! With *how* many pounds of art supplies on your back?"

"Oh, it's going to be a drag," she said. "But I'm not coming back here anytime soon. No way will I leave my stuff behind." I heard her grunt and I knew she was shouldering her pack. "I'm *not* going to let this crunch keep me from starting some kind of art this week. I'm brewing up a new project. . . ." Her voice trailed, then snapped back again. "I'm going to make this interesting. I'm taking I-95 home."

"The highway?"

"Yep. Have you seen it today, Dewey?"

"No. But I can't hear it either. It has to be dead out there," I said.

"Hmm . . . not exactly, Mr. Supersonic," Lil said. "*Everybody's* out there now, either walking or biking. It's pretty surreal," Lil said. Then she mumbled something about wishing she'd biked to the city that morning.

"Really? But isn't being on the highway illegal?"

"Hey, weird times, civilian rule," she said.

"Besides, Dad always says the highway is the fastest. Ha-ha! Now listen, take good care of Angus and Eva, and make me something good for dinner."

"Lil! Wait! Isn't it twenty miles from there to here?"

"Twenty-two. At least I wore comfortable shoes," Lil said. The phone crackled. "Dewey? You there?"

I upped my volume. "Yep. Still here. Hey, Lil, I'm going to come get you," I said. "I'll bring the tandem and—"

"No, no, no. Don't come," Lil said. "Hey, Dew? I can't hear—I think I'm losing you."

Lil is almost always right.

6

I MADE A NEW PLAN. I WAS GOING TO BE HEROIC.

I knew I'd find Vince in the paddock with the dogs. He liked to take a bike stand out and work in "natural light," as he said. Goodness and Greatness thumped their tails at me. Dust rose out of the dry grass. Vince looked up.

"Oh, you're back," he said.

"Yeah. Any more jobs come in?"

"Nope." (Vince usually gives the shortest answer possible.) He grinned with relief.

"Will you help me bring the tandem down?" I asked. He gave me a slightly puzzled look.

We had to move eight different bikes, in for eight different repairs, to get to the wall where our tandem hung on a couple of J-hooks. I took the front end. Vince took the rear.

"To the shoulder on three," I said. "One, two, three." We both grunted. With the bike on my shoulder I paused for a breath and to steady the handlebars. Vince didn't. He set his end down. I lost my balance, then I lost my grip. The wheel turned hard, and my end of the bike took a twisting spill to the ground with me falling onto it. "Ow!" I yelled. The dogs thumped their tails again.

"Sorry," said Vince.

"Never mind." I righted myself and the bike. I grabbed a set of Allen wrenches and reached for the panniers on the shelf above me.

"Wait. Panniers?" Vince said. "You taking a trip?"

"Sort of," I said. "If I'm not here to remind you, don't forget to get Angus and Eva from Sea Camp."

"Where are you going?" Now he was slightly panicked.

"Lil's class got canceled. She's walking the highway home. I'm going to pick her up." I started on my way.

"So I'm on my own? Again?"

I hollered over my shoulder, "Close the Bike Barn door and hide if you can't deal with the people. I'll be back as soon as I can!"

7

ON THE OVERPASS, I STOOD UP ON THE PEDALS
and got my first good look at the highway below.

Surreal, Lil had said. And she was right. Lanes
were forming down there. Walkers on the far right,
bikers to the left of the rumble strip, and speedier
bikers to the left of those. The far left lane was
open on the off chance, I guessed, that something
bigger might come humming through.

I merged onto the highway. Riding a tandem
solo is less awkward than it looks. It's fine once
you get it rolling. Then it has a stretch-limo thing
going for it on the visual. We'd be faster coming
home once I had Lil on the back. Or, knowing Lil,
once she had me on the back. Anyway, I didn't
get too many funny looks because it wasn't long

before I picked up a rider. I passed a guy in a shirt and tie, briefcase swinging at his side. He jogged a few steps and called out, "Whoa! Hey! Hey, kid! Help a guy out? I'm looking at that empty seat! Could we work together?"

I squeezed the brakes and pulled right. It was the only thing to do. I stood astride the tandem and twisted back to look at him. He looked slightly familiar. But more important, he wasn't old, and he looked pretty fit. This could pay off.

"I'm not sure how far I'm going," I said. "Maybe just to the East Elm City line. I'm watching for my sister. She's on foot somewhere in the northbound lane. The trains out of the city were jammed."

"Same with the trains in," he answered with a nod. "Really makes you wonder how long it'll go on. But they say this is all about politics. Not geology," he added.

Geology. I felt like I'd swallowed a spoonful of sand. We'd talked about that at home. I cleared my throat and said, "My dad says politics is just about people not being able to get along. So maybe this'll be over soon. As for geology, well, everybody gets it now, right? World demand will become too high." I shrugged. "My dad thinks we can invent our way out of it if we scramble," I added. "Bring back the electric car."

"I think your dad is right." The guy nodded. "In the meantime, I've had enough walking. Job or no job, I'm going to have to buy a bike."

"Ever ridden a tandem before?" I asked.

"I haven't," he said. "But I've biked. And I learn fast."

"Here, strap your briefcase to the rack." I handed him a bungee from my handlebar bag. "And roll your pants."

"Sorry to hold you up," he said. "This is very nice of you."

"If we do well together, it'll be worth it," I said. "It's important that we start off exactly together. Watch me. You have to *anticipate*," I said. It was a weird way for me to talk to an adult. But I had to make sure he wouldn't make us crash the tandem. "And I can't hold the bike up on my own. Not with your weight on it. So you have to follow my lead. Settle yourself quickly. Other than that, it's not much different from a regular bike. You just don't get to steer. But I'm a safe rider, I promise. Oh, and the pedal cages can be rough on your shoes."

"I remember," he said.

The rear pedal set whacked the guy in the shin and gave him a good skinning at the start. "You'll think of me tomorrow," I said apologetically. A hundred yards later we started to cruise past other cyclists. We were not a bad team.

"This is great!" the guy called up to me. "The speed! Wow! Seems almost unfair!"

By Exit 57 I knew my rider's name was Robert Deal. He'd been out of college just a few weeks and he was job hunting in Elm City.

"I'm trying to impress future employers just by showing up to interview during this shortage," he said.

"So how's that working for you?" I asked.

"It's not! Nobody's hiring. Been thinking about trying to go back to the beach. I was a lifeguard back in high school—"

"Oh!" I said. "At the town beach in Rocky Shores?"

"Yes."

"You once treated me for a jellyfish sting!" I said.

"I did that a lot!" he said.

We biked on. The truck stop at Exit 56 was full of trucks—stuck trucks, which, of course, made me think of Mom and Dad.

"I'm going to slow us down some," I told Robert. "I don't want to miss my sister." I began to wonder if she'd changed her mind about walking the highway. Then just before the frontage-road strip mall, I saw her. "There she is!" I said. "Lil! Lilly Marriss!" I strained. Ridiculous. She'd never hear me. "Look, Robert, I've got to take the off-ramp and get back on again to come up behind her. I can't see us lifting the tandem over the barrier."

"No! That'd be the very moment a truck comes barreling along," he said.

We came to a clean stop.

"I can't thank you enough, Dewey. You saved

35

me miles of walking," Robert said.

"You helped me, too," I said. "Listen, if you think you're really going to buy a bike, my family has a business. Repairs, mostly. But we have a few bikes that we built from parts. They're excellent machines for the money. We guarantee them." I grabbed one of our business cards from the handlebar bag and thrust it at him. I wanted to go catch up to Lil.

Then I heard it. A hum in the distance. It sliced through the sounds of pedals, gears, and voices on the highway like it had a direct line to my ears. I looked to the north. All I could see was the long broken line of bikes and riders, coming down the highway.

The hum grew louder. Then there it was. A single diesel, gleaming in the sun. Every head turned to watch it, every rider braced for the draft. The truck whooshed by. Time stood still for just a beat. Then everyone started moving again.

I turned to Robert and stuck my hand out. "Pleasure biking with you," I said. I shook his hand hard. I swung myself back onto the seat of the tandem. He gave me a running push to start me up the ramp. As I crossed above the traffic I looked down. Tried to find him again. No luck. He must have been hoofing it onward to Elm City.

8

LIL COULDN'T HIDE IT. SHE WAS GLAD TO SEE me in spite of herself. She ran at me and landed me with a bear hug. For the second time that day the tandem twisted to the ground. For the second time I fell on top of it.

I lay there looking up at the sky while the front axel hub stuck into my kidney and Lil cheered, "My taxi cometh! My taxi cometh!" We drew a few grins. Sideshow on the highway.

On the way home, I was right where I figured I'd be: looking at Lil's back. She set us a good pace.

We talked to each other in little shouts as we pedaled. "Well, the class may be canceled, but I am *not* going to sit around," she insisted. "I'm going to put a mural across the back of the small barn."

"A piece of art for Mr. Spivey?" I joked. That wall faced his yard.

"Right! Just for him!" Lil laughed. "Pay him back for the pleasure of looking at his lovely junk pile."

Lil has always been intense about her art. Mom says she goes at it "body and soul," and it's true. She mixes paint, wood, metal—everything and anything she can get her hands on, from old timbers and windows to hinges to horseshoes. I like the stuff my sister makes. One of her best pieces started with something I'd given her.

I'd found a bike out by the highway. It'd been dropped from a car, and probably run over—maybe more than once. It looked like tinfoil. But Lil took all the parts and she mangled and untangled, she hammered and she painted, and she created the coolest piece of kinetic art ever. Since it was pretty much all made out of bike parts, we hung it up over the entrance of the Bike Barn door.

That's where Mrs. Bertalli saw it when she'd brought her sons' bikes to us for tune-ups. She'd gone wild. She'd hired Lil to do a piece for her on the spot. "Anything you want to make," she'd said. "It'll be the focal point for my patio garden. A freestanding sculpture!" That was Lil's first sale.

But the important part is that when Mrs. Bertalli's home had been part of the town garden tour that summer, a big, full-color picture of Lil's work had made it into an article in the *Shoreline Weekly Sun*. (I think Mrs. Bertalli made that happen.) From there, Lil's art had caught on.

Lil and I pulled off the highway and down our driveway. We let the bike down and sat in the shade for just a minute. "So, what if we cook up some bacon and tomatoes with barley tonight?" Lil said.

"Oh my gosh, best thing! I forgot to tell you!" I said. "Pop and Mattie are coming to make chowder tonight."

"You're kidding? Oh yes! Yes! This day doesn't totally stink after all!" she said. She set to unpacking her supplies from the panniers. Then she paused. "This isn't a pity supper, is it?"

"What do you mean?"

"They aren't feeling sorry for us because Mom and Dad aren't home, are they?"

I laughed. "It's *clam chowder*, Lil! Do you care *why* it's coming?" Lil could go overboard on the whole "we can take care of ourselves" thing sometimes. "They had a good dig this morning," I said. "And besides, Pop and Mattie are our friends. They come when Mom and Dad are here too. Plus, we're providing everything but the clams."

"Hmm. Right." Lil gathered up her supplies. "I'm serious, by the way. I'm starting on that mural. Today. Mark my words, there will be art!"

9

IN THE BIKE BARN, VINCE WAS LEANING OVER the workbench in the shop with a pile of pink work orders in front of him. He held a few of them in one hand.

"Oh hey," he said when he saw me. He thought for a second. "You made pretty good time."

"I had help. I picked up a rider on the way out."

Vince grinned. "A *hitchbiker*," he said.

I laughed, wishing I'd thought of it. "So, did it go okay?" I asked.

"Mrs. Bertalli came in," he told me in a slightly stick-it-to-me way.

"No!" I said. I hated that I'd missed her, and my brother knew it.

"Well, you'll see her again," he said. "She left

Chris's and Carl's bikes for work." The boys were rough riders. We saw their bikes often.

"So what else?" I asked. I pointed to the papers in his hand. "What are those? Tough jobs? Do we need Dad for those?"

"Yes. Well, I might be able to do them," Vince said. I thought it was really cool of him not to completely give up. "But it's parts, too."

"Yeah. We don't have them. I'm going to have to take a trip out to Bocci Bike and Rec to buy parts," I said.

Vince grunted.

"Not today," I said. "I've been thinking about this. We need a new system. What's that called when the hospital gets a whole bunch of people in at one time?"

"Bloody?"

"I mean when they have to divide them up. They decide who they can help, like who's critical and who just needs to get patched up—"

"Oh, *triage*!" Vince said.

"That's it. We have to *triage* these repairs."

Vince screwed up his face. "*Organize* them?"

he said, and you'd have thought I'd asked him to roll in poison ivy.

"Look, just take the next order you can do off the top and go start it. I'll sort the rest out. And by the way, sorry about leaving you this morning. I'll take care of everyone who comes in from now on."

Vince glanced at something over my shoulder. "Everyone," he said.

I turned around.

It was our neighbor. Mr. Spivey.

Sometimes Mr. Spivey actually asked for help rather than just helping himself. But even then it was more like being *told* what you were going to do for him. It was even a little like being yelled at about it. So when he said, "I'm going to need you to come over with that push mower today," I understood him. He expected to borrow our mower, but he also expected a boy to come with it.

I remembered to greet him. "Hello, Mr. Spivey," I said. I thought to ask him if he'd enjoyed his sunny-side-up breakfast, but I skipped it. "I'd like to help you," I lied. "But the mower is at a house over on Sandy Reach Road."

He stood with his arms crossed tightly over his chest with his hands in his pits. Familiar stance. Next, he'd fling a hand forward and jab his finger at the ground like a pecking hen.

"Well, when can I expect that back here?" he asked. Sure enough. There was the fling and the peck. He retucked his hands.

"The mower?" I said. "We'd need a truck to get it. And gas. And of course if we had gas, you could run your own mower." That last part might have sounded fresh. But I was just thinking out loud. I was also trying to think what Dad would do.

"I can bring you our sheep, Gloria Cloud," I said as cheerfully as I could. "She'll graze that lawn for you."

Mr. Spivey thought about it. "Fine," he said. "But I'll need the big one instead. That one you've got in the back."

"Sprocket?" I said. "The billy goat?"

Vince muffled a snort and ducked out toward the paddock.

Mr. Spivey went on and I watched his bobbing finger. "The big one will eat more. Faster. I need

45

that lawn taken down," he said.

"Mr. Spivey," I said, "you *really* don't want Sprocket. Billy goats can be bad company. Besides, he's more of a *brush cutter*. Mass destruction. You've seen how he's gnawed a ring in that old pine tree," I added.

He seemed to think it over while he gave me a hard squint. "Right then," he finally said. "The sheep. You bring her over. I'll need the dooryard done first." He turned and walked out.

I looked at the bike-repair orders in my hand. Triage, I thought. I sighed. The sooner I delivered Gloria Cloud, the sooner I'd get back to work. I went out through the paddock. As I passed Vince's work stand he jabbed one finger toward the ground and said, "Now, I'm going to need that grazed on a diagonal."

"Yeah, yeah, yeah," I said. I hoisted myself over the fence in pursuit of Gloria Cloud.

10

IT SEEMED LIKE TEN MINUTES PASSED FROM THE time I tethered Gloria to a cinder block in Mr. Spivey's yard until the time Vince left to get the twins from camp. The day was melting away. I felt a wave of panic. I hadn't done a single repair. I had to get on top of things. Somehow.

I grabbed the next order up. Mr. Gilmartin. He had a pretty upscale bike, but it wasn't brand-new anymore. He really needed a new derailleur, but he'd already told me that he didn't want to spend a lot for it. So I'd promised him I'd work with what was there.

I stood staring at the bike. I was stuck.

Whenever I get hung up on a job in the shop, I check Dad's list of the Eight Rules That Apply to

Fixing Almost Anything. (He also calls it his One-Page Bible for Bike Mechanics.) He keeps it tacked to the Bike Barn wall. It's rumply and all covered in grease spots. And it rarely fails me.

1. **RIGHT IS TIGHT.** True for nuts, bolts, and screws, with few exceptions.

2. **USE PROPER TOOLS FOR THE JOB.**

3. **AN OUNCE OF MAINTENANCE IS WORTH A POUND OF REPAIRS.**

4. **RUST NEVER SLEEPS.** Ask yourself where water might accumulate.

5. **STUDY THE PROBLEM.** Understand how something works before you try to figure out why it isn't operating correctly.

6. **TRY THE LEAST EXPENSIVE FIX FIRST.** It's often the solution.

7. **TAKE NOTES ON COMPLICATED JOBS.** Consider how the thing was assembled in the first place.

8. **ONE REPAIR AT A TIME.** Work on one problem at a time. Disassemble as little as possible.

Reading the rules always reminds me that bikes are pretty simple machines—though that doesn't mean fixing them is always a snap. Mr. Gilmartin had already directed me toward Rule Six—the least expensive fix. So, I went at it and I managed to work it out.

When Vince came back with Angus and Eva, I couldn't help crowing. "I took care of that Gilmartin job," I told him. "And no new derailleur. I worked with what was there. Fixed his flat and his shifter cables, too. One more out the door," I added.

Vince gave me a nod. Not that impressed.

It was a good afternoon. Nobody came to check in a bike during the heat of the day. So Vince and I worked steadily. Angus and Eva spent a while out back with Lil. Then they came in and stomped around the loft above the bike shop.

Every so often I'd look up from the workbench and see a sweaty little face or hand appear at the Trap, as we called it. It was a basketball-size hole in the boards that we kept covered with an old

49

toilet-seat lid on a hinge. The twins loved flipping it open, calling down to us, and dropping things through the hole. A handful of dandelions, three cherry tomatoes, and Angus's left sneaker all rained down on my workbench that afternoon.

Around four or five o'clock customers began to come for their bikes. This was the part I liked. A lot.

"Oh, I'm so glad this place is here," Mr. Chandra told me. He pressed a few extra bills into my hand and I thanked him.

Old Mrs. Marrietta hiked in from the Post Road to pick up her cruiser. "One-stop shopping! I got my eggs, got my wheels. Enough walking for my old hips for today. Biking home will feel like flying! Thank you so much!"

But Dad had warned me: You can't please everyone.

There I was proudly wheeling Mr. Gilmartin's bike out of the shop for him. There he was changing into his biking shoes after probably a four-mile walk. He grinned when he saw his bike again.

"Ahh . . . I sure have missed it," he said.

"Wish we could work faster," I told him. "I think you'll be set for a while longer. It's going through its gears smoothly now. Your limit screws were off and your derailleur cage was bent. You've got new shifter cables, and I put a new inner tube on the front like we talked about. All in all, you still own a great bike." I felt nervous about telling him the next part so I hesitated. "Look, I know that you declined, but I still recommend that new rear derailleur. This one is showing fatigue. The adjustments are temporary."

"Well, I know you tried to talk me into it," he said with a doubtful sort of smile.

"Right. Well you can always let us know if you change your mind."

"The Bike Barn always does good work," he said. We never got tired of that compliment. I handed Mr. Gilmartin his itemized bill. He read the slip and immediately pulled his chin in. He gave me a sharp look. "Seems pretty steep," he said.

"Uh . . . well, parts have gone up," I said. "But maybe I added wrong." I reached for the tab to take a second look. But Mr. Gilmartin was still busy scrutinizing it.

"Since when do shifter cables cost so much?" he wanted to know.

Oh, crud. Here goes.

"W-well, bike parts have . . . uh . . . they've taken a huge hit during the crunch." The words went tripping over my lips.

"So you said." His volume went up. The look on his face could have killed mildew. "But this is *preposterous*," he said.

That's when I felt my limbs drain.

Mr. Gilmartin pressed on. "I know bikes well enough to know that this is something like *triple* what it should be. Same for the lousy derailleur cage. And the tube, too. Is your father here? I want to speak to him."

"H-he's not," I said.

"When will he be back?"

"Uh . . . it's hard to say, Mr. Gilmartin. We've had some bad luck. He's caught up north due to the outage—"

"Then *you're* going to have to explain this to

me." He shoved the tab at me and said, *"I'm not satisfied."*

I gulped. Stick to the facts, I thought. I took a breath. "We actually haven't marked anything up. I'll show you the invoices. We're paying more too. We've kept our labor price at a minimum—"

"I'm not talking about the labor price!" he said. "I'm talking about simple things that don't even have moving parts!"

"Sir, *please* let me show you our costs." Finally, he followed me into the shop. I fumbled with the invoice. I showed him each line item, even though part of me felt like I shouldn't have to. "You are right," I said. "Some costs have tripled."

"I *know* I'm right. I just don't see how it's possible," he said. He whipped his wallet out of his back pocket. "But you have me over a rail, haven't you?" he said. "You *know* I'll pay. I need the bike."

He *did* pay. Practically threw the bills at me.

I walked him back outside. "We appreciate your business, Mr. Gilmartin. If you have any problems . . . well, we guarantee our work."

He never answered me.

I leaned on the fence, waiting for my hollow limbs to fill again. "Well, that sure stunk," I said to myself.

"Hey, Dew." Lil had come around from her side of the barn. She was covered in smudges—the sign of a good art day.

"Hey," I said. I flapped Gilmartin's bills against the fence rail.

"I've seen some happy people pedaling out of here," she said. "Good job." Then she called for Angus and Eva, who came running out of the shop as I went back inside.

"Happy . . . except for that last one," I mumbled.

I didn't want to tell Lil much about the Bike Barn. She had her thing to be in charge of while Mom and Dad were away, and I had mine. Of course it was in the back of my mind that Lil was ultimately in charge of Everything Marriss. The Bike Barn fell under that bigger umbrella and I knew she felt that way too. But as long as there were no problems, that wouldn't come up.

Gilmartin had paid and he was gone. I popped the lid off our peppermint tin. Couldn't help but take a whiff. It still smelled of peppermints every time I opened it. There was a pretty good roll of bills in there, and I added Gilmartin's to the coil. I was going to have to make another bank deposit soon. Dad had taught me how, and I liked biking up to the drive-through window. But I also liked another picture that I held in my mind: us kids handing Mom and Dad a good wad of cash—all from the Bike Barn—when they got home. Okay, *me* handing them the wad. Whatever. I just wanted them to know I'd done it; I'd kept the shop going with no major troubles.

I set the tin on the back of the workbench. I leaned around the door to the paddock. "Vince," I called, "you coming to help me with the pit fire? It's time."

I was up for a huge meal. And no grouch was going to sour my chowder.

11

"THEY'RE HERE!" I HEARD LIL SING OUT.

I looked up from the coals. Pop Chilly and Mattie were coming down our driveway. Pop pedaled his seniorcycle, as he called it—a big green tricycle with a tractor seat and a huge wire basket on the back—into the yard. Mattie rode her pale blue cruiser (with her new tire) and a creel on the front. She had her backpack on, and two long loaves of bread stuck up out of it behind her head.

Lil ran to greet them. She was happy to see Pop and Mattie, but she was still mad about her class being called off. "But I'm starting something here," I heard her say as I got closer. "I'm not giving up just because of this rotten crunch."

Suddenly Pop called out, "Oh boy, here it comes! Quadruple trouble!" Goodness and

Greatness came wagging. Angus and Eva followed. They climbed straight up onto Pop Chilly's
seniorcycle.

"Hello, stinkers!" Pop said. "Don't tip me
over!" (Impossible. The trike was as stable as a
mountain. The thing had *running boards*.) Pop
took one twin onto each knee and hugged them
up. Old Goodness stood by politely woofing under
his breath while Greatness licked Pop's ankle.

"What's that on my foot?" Pop said.

"That's Greatie's tickle torture," Angus said.

Mattie laughed. "We'd have to debate who's
being tortured there, I think." She shrugged her
way out of her backpack. I stepped up to take it
from her and the smell of French bread reached all
the way down to my hungry gut.

"Hey, hey!" Vince called. He came striding out
of the house with a jug of iced tea and set it on the
picnic table.

"Hey, hey, yourself!" Mattie called back.

Pop Chilly hefted the clam bucket down from
the trike before any of us could offer to help.
"Strong as an ox, I am," he said, and it was true.

Lil set to chopping onions. Pop sat scrubbing

potatoes over a bucket while Eva clung to his back and talked in his ear. Mattie, Vince, and I set to checking the clams for a tight seal.

Twice I had to stop, wash seawater off my hands, and log in bikes for repairs. "Is there any chance I can pick up tomorrow morning?" one guy asked. Vince rolled his eyes at me from behind the guy's back.

We had the onions sizzling in the bacon fat when one more person arrived. But this guy didn't bring a broken bike with him. He came dragging in on foot like a lost dog come off the highway. But he wasn't lost. He meant to be right where he stood, five feet in front of me.

"Dewey," he said. "Dewey Marriss. Do you remember me?" He held up a Marriss Bike Barn business card in one hand, and I knew I ought to know him. But his face was tomato red from the heat. His shirt was soaked at the pits and open at the neck. His sleeves and pant legs were rolled to catch the breeze. I looked at the raw, purple scrape on his shin.

"Dewey," he said. "I need to buy that bike."

"Oh!" I said. "Robert Deal!" I turned to Vince and said, "Hey, it's my *hitchbiker*."

12

I INTRODUCED ROBERT DEAL TO EVERYONE. Well, more like I explained who he was, and he and Mattie recognized each other from the beach a few years back. But I couldn't help thinking that he was not quite the same Robert that I'd met on the highway that morning. That Robert was a pretty cool lifeguard dude. This guy was burned toast. Then I realized he must have just walked twenty-something hot miles from Elm City. I think he was trying to smile at us. But his lips stuck to his teeth and made him look like a ferret.

Pop poured a glass of iced tea and held it out to Robert. "Drink this, son. Down the hatch. Right now. Whole thing."

Robert obeyed, taking gulp after gulp. He

looked like a fish trying to put out a fire in its own belly.

"We should dunk him in the trough," mumbled Pop.

"I dunked in the trough once," said Angus.

"Yeah," Eva said. "And remember? Mom said, 'Angus! Ahhh! The trough is not for boys!'" Eva waved her hands over her head. I thought Pop was going to fall over.

Robert looked up at us between swallows of tea. I felt bad for him. All of us were laughing, though not at him, and now, a salt-hungry Marriss dog was going in for a lick on his bare leg.

"Greatie! Leave him!" I called. But Robert leaned down to pat her before he took another drink.

Lil piped up, "Mr. Deal, are you all right?"

Robert swallowed and tried to catch his breath. "Y-yes. And hello," he said. "You're Lilly. I saw you in the morning. I mean, across the highway lanes. When I rode on the back of Dewey."

Vince let out a laugh. I shot him a look, but I couldn't really blame him for thinking it was funny. Robert made it sound like I'd carried him piggyback down the highway.

Robert looked at Lil and tried again. "Sorry. I mean, when Dewey *gave* me a ride."

Lil helped him out. "You rode the tandem."

"Yes. But tonight, I-I need to buy a bike," Robert said. He held up our business card again.

Lil got up from the table where she'd been chopping potatoes. "Okay then," she said. "But it's dinnertime and—"

No, no, no, I thought. Don't go being the parents now . . . oh, she's going to turn him away. . . .

"I'm really sorry. I should have realized . . ." Robert said.

"It's okay. What I was going to say is, Dewey will help you with the bike. But not until you've cooled off, and not before we've all had supper. Together. We'll set another place."

Okay, yes. Be the parents, Lil. You go! She sounded just like Mom and Dad, actually.

"Oh, no. I can't do that," Robert said.

"People come here for dinner all the time," Angus said.

"True that," said Mattie. "*I* sure do!"

"And me!" Pop raised his hand.

"You can stay," said Eva. "I'll even get another bowl."

I turned to Robert. "There's a shower around the back of the house. It's private. You can cool off and—"

"I'll find you something to wear. We've got a stash of old clothes in the basement," said Lil.

"He has that over-hotness disease, doesn't he?" Angus said, leaning toward Pop's ear. Just about everything the twins said made Pop laugh out loud.

I took Robert around the back of the house as much to rescue him from my family and friends as to show him where the shower was. I grabbed a clean towel from the clothesline and threw it to him. "I'll bring the clothes and leave them on the hook."

"Thanks," he said. "I'm sorry for interrupting your dinner."

"That's okay," I said. "No problem."

"Okay, careful with the heat now," Mattie said. Vince and I knocked the fire down. We slid the heavy pot over the grate. Mattie's secret to great chowder was leaving the shells in. I liked the sound of them scraping against the pot.

"Won't be much longer now," she said.

Robert Deal came around from the back of the house looking less like a human tomato. He wore a loose T-shirt and a pair of cargo shorts that he had to hike up with just about every step.

Lil looked him over. "Eh, maybe a little big. Best I could do." She shrugged. "Feel better, Mr. Deal?"

"Yes," he said. "But will all of you just call me Robert? Please."

"Robert. Have a seat," said Lil. "Angus, Eva, pass those napkins."

Vince and I grabbed the bowls and held them while Mattie filled each one with chowder, shells and all. We set them around the table and Lil dropped a lump of butter off a knife into each one.

"Enjoy that butter, friends," she said. "There won't be any more until we get to the grocery store. And who knows how that'll go in these new weird times," she added. There was a collective nod all around the table. But it was a nod that said more about enjoying that lump of butter *now* than it did about how long it'd be before we had another one. I had been missing Mom and Dad at dinnertime more than any other part of the day. It was good to have a crowd around the table.

"You break bread, son." Pop Chilly gave Robert a nudge.

"That's because you're the guest," Eva told him.

"No. It's because you have the cleanest hands," Pop said.

Robert fell right in, handing hunks of bread around the table. He looked at his bowl of chowder and said, "Spoons?"

"Ah. It's done like this," said Mattie. She picked a clamshell out of her bowl and scooped it full of chowder. She closed her eyes, tipped everything into her mouth, and slurped.

Bad manners ruled. We all slurped. We all dabbed our hunks of French bread into puddles of the chowder and we all licked our fingers. We clinked shells in our bowls and tossed empties into the tin colander in the center of the picnic table. We were consumed with consuming.

I might have been on my second-to-last clam when I realized that something had changed. Something had been added. I *felt* it behind me. It was Mr. Spivey.

"I'll need one of you to come get that sheep out of my yard now."

I turned on the bench. There he stood, just ten feet away, hands in his pits. I had probably missed the pecking finger.

I found my wits and said, "Okay, Mr. Spivey. I'll be there in about fifteen minutes." I think we all must have been staring at him then.

The Spive shook his head. "Can't wait, can't keep watch that long," he said.

Pop Chilly tossed an empty clamshell into the colander with a bang. He looked right at the Spive. "I heard the young man say he'd be there soon. We're enjoying a well-earned supper here."

"What's that you say?" Mr. Spivey sometimes pretended he was hard-of-hearing.

Pop Chilly raised his volume. "I said, *not quite done with supper*!"

"Shh! Pop!" Mattie touched her father's arm. "Settle down."

"I'm settled!" Pop growled. "This is communication. This is how it's done—geezer to geezer."

Then, because timing is everything, our own Officer Runkle came biking down the drive with another Rocky Shores bike cop right behind him— somebody new. The Spive scuttled away around the fence into his own yard.

"Hello, fine Marrisses and fine Marriss friends!" Officer Runkle called. (He did some community theater on the side. Mom always admired the depth of his voice. "He's a bit like a town crier," she said.)

"Hey, Runks!" Lil waved one arm over her head.

"And how are you this warm summer eve?" Runks asked.

"Stuffed!" Pop Chilly called.

"Runks, I'm afraid we didn't leave you or the other officer a single clam," said Lil. She gave the new guy a wave and he returned it.

"Not to worry," he said. He stood astride his copsicle and patted his gut. "We've already dined, thanks. I'm really here to introduce you to our recruit. Say hello to Officer Macey."

A few things about the new cop stood out. First, he seemed young for a cop—about the same age as our new friend Robert, I figured. Second, he had that white-blond hair. The kind that looks like it's glowing in the dark even when it's daylight. And finally, he was a beast. Biker muscles, big-time.

"I thought Macey should get to know you," Runks said. "He's on bike duty for now. Fast as lightning, he is."

I believed it. It'd be fun, I thought, to get him out on the highway and just try and keep up. But it wasn't like I had time on my hands.

Runks turned to Officer Macey. "The Marriss Bike Barn is the nearest and dearest stop when a cable snaps or the gears turn rickety. These are good people to know," he said.

"We'll put you ahead of our orders and get you

back on the road," I told him. "Just like we do for Runks."

"I do most of my own maintenance and repairs," said Macey. "But thanks. I'm still glad to know you're here."

Dad would like that, I thought. He always said it just made sense to be able to do at least minor fixes on any machine you own.

"So how goes the bike-repair biz in these days of fewer carbon emissions?" asked Officer Runkle.

"Busy," I said. "Vince and I are working overtime."

"Slaves," said Vince. "Child labor. Call the authorities. Oh wait, you *are* the authorities, aren't you?"

Eva sat forward. "Officer Runks, did you know that Dad and Mom went away? They can't get back to our house because the pumps dried up," she said. "So did the diesel and that's how my dad's truck runs."

"Oh, no kidding?" said Runks. He looked at Lil and then at me.

"But they're going to keep calling us every night," Eva said.

Pop Chilly slipped an arm around Eva. He planted a kiss on her head. "That's right," he said.

"How long have they been out?" Runks asked Lil.

"Well, they're just a day past the plan so far," said Lil. "Dad thought the ration cards would be a sure thing, you know?"

Runks shook his head. "This shortage has caught all of us."

"Have you seen the highway?" I asked.

Officer Macey made a loud laugh. "Seen it? That's all we do. Bike in big circles all day and the highway's one of our major loops. The staties can't cover it all."

"I biked out there today," I said. "Oh. Not to get myself in trouble . . ." I grimaced and ducked my head.

"We're not making arrests for just walking or riding out there," Macey said. "Too much paper-work!"

"Then I confess too!" Robert stood and shook

hands with both officers. "Yes, sirs! I'm guilty of many hot, illegal miles on foot. I'm buying a bike. Tonight. Tomorrow, I join the pedaling violators."

"That's cool," Officer Macey said. "Just watch out. It's bound to get nasty out there eventually."

"Really? You mean road rage?" I said. "I thought everything was pretty orderly. Lanes forming and all."

"Sure. For now. But it's hot and people will get frustrated, and they'll turn mean." Macey folded his arms over his chest and nodded.

"Where? Who's being mean?" Angus wanted to know.

Pop cleared his throat loudly. Both Angus and Eva had saucer eyes trained on Macey. Runks shifted. He shook his head at Macey, who quickly said, "Oh, sorry about that."

Robert Deal spoke up. "Well, people have been nothing but nice to me. Dewey gave me a ride this morning. That was the best help I've had. But I've seen other good things happening in recent days."

"Like what?" Lil asked.

"Well, this afternoon, some of the businesses

and residences that back up to the highway set up rest stops. Places in the shade with lawn chairs. They leave their hoses out. Of course only the *smart* people use them." He grinned and pointed to himself. "I should have. Obviously. One of the motels in Sand Orchard was letting people dunk their feet in the pool. For free!" Robert smiled at the twins. "People are *good*," he said. He reached across the table and tapped Eva on the nose. "I've made new friends on the highway."

"Our dad and mom are making friends too. Where they are." Eva said. We didn't know this to be true, so I thought it was funny that Eva said it. She pointed in exactly the direction our parents had gone.

"Hey, when are they going to call?" Angus asked.

"Probably just before bedtime," Lil said. "Let's clear and start the dishes. We'll have dessert later."

"I love doing dishes!" said Angus.

"Me too," said Eva.

This was true. They loved standing on chairs

at the kitchen sink. They also loved using *way* too much soap.

"I'll help," said Mattie. She started stacking our empty bowls. "I can't stand to sit still anyway."

"Well, I can!" said Pop Chilly. "I'm going to sit right here doing my imitation of a well-fed old man." He thumped his belly. "Unless you want me to go get that sheep from the geezer neighbor," Pop said.

"Oh, Gloria Cloud," I said. I jumped up.

"No, Dewey, you have a customer," Lil said. "I'll go get Gloria Cloud from our fine neighbor, who, by the way, spent the day following our woolly girl around his yard with a shovel."

"A shovel!" Mattie looked horrified. "Why?"

"Because he doesn't want any of her manures," Angus said.

"Fear of feces," Vince said, and Robert coughed to cover a laugh.

"He catches the manures on the shovel. Then he puts them over in our yard," Eva said.

"Wait," said Officer Macey. "Are you talking about the guy I saw slinking around here when we rode up? A guy with a weird walk?"

"Yes. Mr. Spivey is a grumpus," Eva leaned forward and whispered.

"Yeah, and he's a thief, too," Angus piped.

"A thief?" Macey said. He squinted at Angus.

Vince shrugged. "Yeah. But he's *our* thief."

"The fine neighbor is prone to petty egg thefts and such," Runks explained. He kept his town crier voice low. "The Marrisses are rather good to him in spite of it."

"Too good!" Pop piped up.

"Never mind," Lil said, flapping a hand.

"So Robert, are you ready?" I tipped my head toward the barn.

"Yes," he said. "Thank you all for dinner. You've been incredibly kind." He gave me a nod. "To the barn," he said.

I led the way.

13

RUNKS AND MACEY CAME WITH US TO THE BIKE
Barn that night. Goodness and Greatness came,
nosing and licking at our guests. Robert leaned
down to pat them on the way. Macey too. With
Runks chatting and doing his town-crier thing, I
felt like I was in a play. I had the role of Dad, wel-
coming everyone into the bike shop.

Runks paused and slapped a hand on the door
to the shop. "Listen, you are locking up after
dark, correct?" he asked. His face was unusually
serious.

"W-well, yeah," I said. "Pretty much." I shot
a look at Vince as if to ask him, *Have we been?* It
wasn't something we'd worried about a lot.

"They're okay," Macey said. "Who's going to

find this place way back here?"

"Oh, they find us," Vince said. I rolled the door open and he pointed at the dozen or so bicycles packed against the south wall.

"Oh." Macey laughed. "I guess they do find you!"

Vince crossed through the shop and pushed open the paddock door. "The overflow," he said. Six or seven more bikes loosely chained up.

Now Runks let out a long whistle. "Whew! Home alone *and* keeping shop, too. Good for you, men! But just a warning, bikes are a commodity these days. Worth more than cash in some ways. We're seeing a lot of thefts," he said.

I nodded, his words settling into the back of my mind.

"So it's pretty much all repairs here?" Officer Macey asked. I think he was trying to lighten things up. He looked around, took our shop in with an approving sort of nod that gave me a huge sweep of pride.

"We don't carry much merch," I said. "A few racks and tubes." I headed up the loft stairs and

everyone followed. "We had to move the bikes we've built up here when the shop filled up with repair jobs."

Robert was the last one up the loft stairs, and he turned to look back at Goodie and Greatie. Both dogs had stopped at the bottom and stood wagging their tails.

"They only climb carpeting," Vince explained.

We just had a few Marriss-built bikes to sell. Dad had sold some the week before the anniversary trip. It didn't take Robert long to zero in on a hybrid.

"It's a good choice," I said. "It's no racer, but it'll do you well for the kind of riding you're doing."

"Nice components," Officer Macey said, looking the bike over. "*Real* nice."

"The Marrisses know how to put together a superior ride," Runks announced, and I figured both he and Macey were good for business.

While Robert and I talked, the officers milled around. They took a look at our little inventory together, then moved off into the loft. At some point, I heard Macey mutter, "Oh, this guy has

got to learn some manners."

I looked up. Macey was at the open hay door looking down into Mr. Spivey's yard. He was shaking his head.

I crossed the loft and looked out. Below us, Lil spoke.

"Mr. Spivey, I'm *not* coming back to shovel up manure and neither are my brothers. The next good rain will take care of it. Trust me." She tugged Gloria Cloud's tether and changed her tone. "Come on, sweet girl," she said.

"The job's not done anyway," Mr. Spivey said, his finger jabbing at the ground. "The grass is still tall in the back! I'm gonna need—"

"*Hey! Enough!*" Macey boomed like thunder. "You hear me? You asked someone to come get the animal and she's done that," he said. "Don't let me hear you say another thing—unless it's thank you."

Fat chance. We didn't get thank-yous out of the Spive. Ever.

"Are we clear?" Macey called down.

Our neighbor retreated to his back porch without answering. We heard the door slam.

I knew *I* was clear—clear that being friends with two cops was going to be even better than being friends with one. Maybe he was a little gruff. But I liked Officer Macey.

We took a short ride out to the highway. It was a great way for Robert to get a feel for his new bike. I got my chance to chase Macey—just a little. He set a good pace. Just when I thought I might pass him, the siren on his copsicle sounded a sharp *Whoop! Whoop!*

"Busted!" he called. "Speeding!" I dropped back behind him, laughing.

Meanwhile, Robert pedaled up beside me and said, "Oh yeah! It's a deal, Dewey! I have found my ride!"

A net of darkness began to fall. Runks and Macey lit our way. Their bike lights were as bright as a car's headlights.

When we stopped back in our yard, the copsicle lights shone on the Bike Barn door. Angus and Eva ran through the beams. Their shadows shrank and grew against the old boards.

"See my wings!" cried Eva. "I'm a bird!"

"I'm a dino!" Angus shouted. Then Goodness's shaggy dog shadow loped in from the side, followed by Greatness's sleek one. Angus's shadow ran away then came back again carrying a branch. "A tree! A tree for your bird, Eva!" He put the branch over his head.

"Do that again, Angus!" Lil called. "That's beautiful!" She put her curled hands up to her eyes like a pair of binoculars. I'd seen her do it before. I knew she was *seeing* something for her art.

Since Runks and Macey were heading back toward town they agreed to escort Pop and Mattie home.

"See you at camp tomorrow morning," Mattie said to the twins.

"Just like . . . yesterday!" Angus said.

"And like today," Eva added.

Meanwhile, Robert Deal paid me in cash and I added the money to our fancy cash register. I duct-taped a flashlight to his handlebars and Vince clipped a reflector onto the back of his shirt.

"We can't have you getting hit by another biker," I said, and I forced a chuckle. I wasn't sure it was funny, but Robert gave me a grin.

"Boy, am I glad I stopped you on that tandem today," he said. He swung up onto his new bike and began to roll.

"Come back anytime!" I called after him as he rode away. "And get a helmet! *Tomorrow!*"

He waved and I heard him call, "Thanks, Dewey!"

Robert was just down the driveway and out of sight when I heard the telephone ringing inside our house. I pushed the barn door closed and squeezed the padlock until it clicked. Then I ran for the phone.

"Is everyone staying healthy? Are you eating all right?" Dad asked. Together he and Mom asked a thousand questions about us kids, especially the twins. "We're fine!" Lil said. "Today wasn't any different than yesterday." That part was sad when it came to Lil personally. Mom and Dad were sorry to learn that her class in Elm City was off.

"It's just unlucky," Lil said, but again, I knew she was toughing it out. She covered by launching into the news that she was starting the new mural, and

I heard her ask Mom about some paint, and Dad something about using the compressor to spray-paint.

I could only assume she meant the same compressor that we used in the bike shop *every day* to pump flats and blow gunk out of bearing sets. The *only* compressor. I scrunched my brow at Vince. He let a puff of air through his lips and whispered, "Kiss that baby good-bye."

But soon Lil was asking about Mom and Dad. "We want to know how *you* are," Lil told them. We all crowded up to listen.

"We're all right," Mom said. "Still sleeping in the tent and paying for showers at the truck stop. There are other people in our same situation. The stops to the south must be much more crowded. So maybe we're lucky that way. They let us charge up the phone, and we watch the news at the diner here. And boy, no rain in sight, huh?" She asked about the garden and the goat girls, but then she asked about us again and again.

Mom relaxed a little when we said we'd seen Pop and Mattie and that we'd eaten a big supper together, and Runks had visited. We put the twins on the phone. They passed the receiver back and forth. I kept hearing Angus say, "But do you think there will be some diesel *tomorrow*?"

Finally, I got a turn to talk and I told Dad about selling the bike to Robert Deal. "Oh, well done!" he said. "Was it busy again today?"

"It was," I said, and I flashed on the Gilmartin incident for a split second. "But nothing we can't handle," I added. Vince threw himself in front of my face and crossed his eyeballs at me. He pretended to choke himself and die on the floor right there in the kitchen. I turned my back on him. "I can't even remember, but I think seven or eight bikes went back out today," I said. "And Dad, I'm probably going to have to make a run to Bocci's for parts soon. How do we usually pay him? Can I take him cash?"

"Sure. Bocci likes cash just fine," Dad said. "But Dewey, what are you running out of? Has there really been that much business?"

"Dad," I said, "it is so cool. We're the ones putting everybody back on the road."

14

THE NEXT MORNING, ANGUS AND EVA AND I pedaled to Sea Camp as usual, except that I had hitched the carrier to my bike. I had a roll of dough in my pocket and I was going to pick up parts at Bocci Bike and Rec. There were just too many jobs in the shop that we couldn't do because we needed this part or that part.

With the twins settled at camp, I cooked down the Post Road and got on the highway at Featherbed Lane. We were in for another hot one. The empty carrier wheeled along easily behind me. I'd be using my legs—big-time—all the way home. For now, I rode the left lane, passing pretty much everyone. I couldn't help thinking, Eat my dust!

Timing is everything. A pack of cyclists on road

bikes began to pass me on the left. They zipped by in their purple-and-white jerseys, heads and shoulders bent over their handlebars.

"Team Bocci!" I whispered to myself. I pedaled harder—for about a nanosecond. Then I watched as they continued down the highway. Talk about dust. They were soon out of view. I'd see them at the store. But not for a while.

I pedaled on. I listened for diesels. One tiny electric surprised me as it hummed by. I had to smile. They were cute, efficient cars. Dad had said we'd be seeing more of them. Vince called them wheelie pods. Around our house, the name had stuck.

Poor Vince. I'd left him alone in the shop again. "Just like yesterday . . ." he'd sort of sung it to me as I was leaving. I'd told him, "We can't clear bikes if we don't have parts."

I followed several other riders into the parking lot at Bocci. No cars.

"Ah, young Mr. Marriss!" Mr. Bocci had an Italian accent that rang like a welcome bell. "And with a trailer, I see." He held the door open while two people rode brand-new bikes right out of the showroom onto the sidewalk.

"Hey, Mr. Bocci," I said. Then, because it seemed the natural thing to say, I asked, "How are sales?"

"Good." He wiped his brow. "*Terribly* good!" He laughed. "You want a job?" He was probably kidding. I wasn't even sure it was legal for a fourteen-year-old kid to have a real job.

"Uh, well, thanks. But we're *terribly busy*, too." I stole his line. "I'm looking for parts, if you can help me," I said. "I tried to get here early. I know you're busy. But I'm on my own—well, with my brother. My dad is stranded up north."

"Yes, yes." His brow creased. "This is the kind of news I hear. Come on in, young Mr. Marriss." He led me to the back of the shop.

As he read the list he gave it a few sharp whacks with the side of his pen. "Okay. Yes-yes. I have these crank sets. Oh, these . . . not sure. We'll check this model. Brake shoes, no problem."

A couple of the mechanics looked up to say hello. They knew me. Sort of. I'd been in with Dad before, back in the days of free-flowing gasoline. Now I tried not to look like the annoying kid down from Rocky Shores just wanting to grab up parts.

Most of Team Bocci's riders were either in sales or worked as mechanics. A couple of those guys hadn't even gotten out of their purple cycling jerseys, but already they were working on bikes. Tools flashed. Wheels spun. They were fast and good at what they did.

"Ack, they will ruin the uniforms," Mr. Bocci muttered. "Degreaser. Lubricants. All petroleum products, you know?" Mr. Bocci handed me an empty cardboard box. He began pulling items from the shelves. "A carton of twenty-seven-inch tubes . . . just one of this twelve-speed gear set . . . Oh, yes. My last one." He plunked it into my box.

"Mr. Bocci," I said. He stopped and looked at me. "Maybe . . . maybe I shouldn't take it then. If it's your last one. It's going to be hard for all of us to get parts now."

"Yes-yes. So this one goes on a bike you fix, or a bike my guys fix. What's the difference? Not to worry," he said. "There will be a way to get more parts. For clever people, the world does not stand still."

I thought for a moment. Hadn't Dad said

something like that just the other night?

"You know the team?" Mr. Bocci went on.

"Your team, sir? The bike racers?"

"Yes. They don't just *ride* for Bocci. They *work* for Bocci. So times change. So maybe I need them to ride to Elm City. Pick up some parts for me there. We are looking to get deliveries off the train. The other shops are going to do the same." He thought for a moment. "It's simple. These teams of riders can meet each other. Pull the trailer like you do. We can hand things off all the way across the country if we have to."

"Y-you mean like the old Pony Express?" I felt my eyebrows rise.

He laughed. "Yes! Sure! But on bikes!"

"Seems *primitive*," I said.

"Going *back* isn't going *backward*. Not if it's the only way to keep going *forward*." Mr. Bocci waited. Maybe he knew that I needed a beat to let that sink in. I liked what he was saying even if it made my brain ache. "Okay, young Mr. Marriss . . ." Mr. Bocci paused again. "I am thinking. And what I am thinking is that you should put as many parts as you can into your shop. How about we pack this box a bit tighter? Maybe it saves you another trip. Then if you don't use these, I take them back."

I hesitated over some of the high-end stuff he was putting in there. Most of our customers wouldn't need that kind of performance. But I didn't want to seem rude, either. In the end I peeled him off most of the bills I had with me. Sort of a shock, but I'd seen Dad spend for parts before too. Mr. Bocci printed me a receipt.

"Do check the prices of parts, young Mr. Marriss," Mr. Bocci warned. "Everything has gone up. *Terribly up*. Don't cheat yourself. You can carry all of this out to your bicycle, yes-yes?"

I almost said yes-yes back, but I caught myself. "Yes, sir, I'm sure I can." I stacked the boxes and got under them to lift them from the counter.

"Bike carefully," Mr. Bocci said. He smiled warmly. "Regards to the Bike Barn!"

I thanked him and went on my way.

15

VINCE HAD AT ME WHILE I RESTOCKED OUR shelves. I let him vent.

"You're supposed to be here," he said. "*You're* the manager. The *people* person. That guy Jerrod came in to get his bike. I had to deliver the bad news. He thinks I'm an idiot," Vince said. "Doesn't believe me that he'll never get that seat post to move again."

I shook my head. "I loaded that thing with penetrating oil. He can try pulling it with a tractor. It's a bimetallic weld. Could have been avoided with a little lube. Rule Three." I reached up to tap a finger on Dad's One-Page Bible for Bike Mechanics. "'An ounce of maintenance is worth a pound of repairs.'"

"Not my point," Vince said.

"I know. But I had to go get these parts." I stepped back from the shelves. "Didn't we have a box of fourteen-gauge spokes? Vince, are you craving metals or something? Are you *eating* bike parts?" I tried to joke, but he just gave me a dirty look in return. I think he thought I was trying to change the subject. "Look," I told him, "I'll be here now. I promise."

"You boys fighting?" Lil popped her head into the shop. She was carrying a bucket of rags and two cans of old paint, and she had several big brushes tucked under her arm.

"No," said Vince. "One of us is *slaving* and one of us is *telling lies*."

"Well, cut it out," she said, but not like she really cared. She didn't even stay long. She was on her way out to work on her mural. I hadn't gone to see it, but I knew she'd been inching a scaffold along the side of the barn so she could reach the higher parts. It was huge fun for Angus and Eva, who loved to climb. They'd been talking about how soon they'd be able to climb the scaffold and make it into the loft through the hay door.

It was probably eleven o'clock before I got on a roll. That was also about the time Vince dropped everything and went fishing. He had a job that had been giving him trouble all morning. I heard him swear in the paddock. Twice. He left a bike on the stand with the pedal set all apart. He tied his rod and tackle to his own bike and started away.

"You'll remember to pick up the twins at camp?" I called after him.

He didn't speak. Didn't turn around. He stuck out one arm, put a thumb up and kept pedaling away.

I wasn't mad. He was sick of the shop and I knew it. There was no denying I would've loved to go hang my toes off the pier too. But we had sixteen bikes in and somebody had to be the *embodiment of responsibility*.

Too bad for Vince, just after he left, Mrs. Bertalli and her boys, Chris and Carl, arrived to pick up their bikes. I'd fudged the order of things just the littlest bit and had pushed them through. She was one of our favorite customers. Lil felt the same way about her. She'd called Mrs. Bertalli "the patron saint of my art."

"Hey, hey, Mrs. B!" I called.

"Hi, Dewey, sweetheart." She waved. Then she stood outside the Bike Barn door gazing up at Lil's smashed bicycle art while I wheeled her boys' bikes out. Chris and Carl shouted, "Hooray! Pedal power!" They rode past the paddock, then out of sight as the pasture sloped downward.

I gave Mrs. Bertalli her invoice. She dug into the straw bag she carried on her handlebars and handed me a large bill. "This will do it," she said. "The extra is a tip. Go spend it when the trucks finally make it to Shoreland's Market."

"Trucks. I'm looking forward to that," I said. I explained that Mom and Dad were gone.

Mrs. Bertalli gasped. "You're *alone*? Oh, I had no idea!"

"Oh, we're fine. We talk to them every night. If they can find a way, they'll put Mom on a train back," I said. "But they're so far north that just getting her to one is a huge problem."

"I saw a *maddening* report that they're selling

train tickets two days ahead. Then not letting people on anyway! It's dreadful. I'm so sorry."

"Thanks, but Dad has trucker's ration cards. When there's gas again they'll be first in line," I said. "Anyway, Lil is here all day. Did you know her art session's been canceled?"

"Oh no! Her scholarship! Poor girl!"

"She's keeping busy," I said. "She's painting around the other side of our barn."

"Dewey, if there's anything you need while your parents are gone— Oh! I almost forgot! I brought a gift." Mrs. Bertalli reached into the straw bag again and grinned. "Now, you can't get these just anywhere anymore. Certainly not at Shoreland's Market . . ." She brought her hand out of the bag slowly.

Roundish. Yellow.

"Lemons!" I said. "You have lemons!" Then I remembered her little potted trees. Vince and I had helped move them out to her patio in the spring.

"Not many!" Mrs. B said. "Who knew lemons would be so rare this summer? I'm thinking of increasing my *orchard*," she said.

"You know what?" I said. "You should take those around back and give them to Lil before you go," I said. "She *loves* lemons."

Later on, Lil poked her nose into the shop—while holding the two lemons up to her eyes, of course. "So where's Vince?" she asked.

"He fritzed out and went fishing," I said.

"Oh." She sighed. "Well, he's not you, Dew."

The way she said it made me feel ridiculously proud. I love it when someone recognizes that I *am* the oldest Marriss brother. "Yeah, I can't blame him for wanting to get out."

Lil was silent. She looked around the shop and out at the bikes in the paddock.

"What?" I said. I drew a length of cable through my hand to relax the curl. My job was waiting.

"I don't know," she said. "This seems like a lot of bikes."

"Hey, weird times," I said, throwing her back her own line. "This is a real business now, Lil."

"Yeah . . ." She had a worried look on her face. I suddenly wanted her to move on. "Dew, can you really handle all these repairs? Are these easy fixes or—"

"We're just jammed up." I spoke louder than I'd meant to. "B-because we didn't have parts until this morning. Besides, once Dad gets back we'll clear them out in no time."

Lil left without saying anything more. I struggled to thread that cable for the next twenty minutes. That never happens. I finally threw it down and went to sit in front of the fan with the dogs. "Where's the Bike Genius and his magic fingers when I need him?" I said. The dogs thumped their tails. A few minutes later, I was trying the cable again.

Dad always says that patience will be rewarded. Mine was. Twice. I won my war with the cable, *and* supper that night was a sizzling batter-dipped sea bass. With lemon. Caught by Vince, cleaned and cooked by Lil. She was just about in her glory squeezing juice from Mrs. Bertalli's lemons over her fish and humming as she ate each bite. But other than that, things were a little quiet at the table.

I took a forkful of the sea bass. "Going fishing was a good idea," I said. Vince looked up from his plate and gave me a guilty look.

"About that . . ." he said.

"I've been thinking," I said. "Do you want to do both trips to Sea Camp?"

"You kidding? I'll do the milking early. I'll be in the shop by nine thirty."

"Deal," I said.

"Umm . . . umm." Lil swallowed another bite of her sea bass. "Nicely negotiated, boys. But we also have to find time for Vince to go fishing again. Soon! Even if we don't have lemons." She paused to put a whole wedge in her mouth.

Eva's face puckered up. "Oh! Lil! I can't eat a lemon like that." She grabbed the sides of her cheeks.

Lil gave Eva a lemon-slice grin.

Eva shook her head at Lil. "Mom says you'll ruin the *ee-nanimal* off your teeth!"

Timing is everything. The phone rang. Mom and Dad were messaging in early. They'd had word that there was a government-aid truck out on the highway.

"Aid trucks? What kind of aid?" I asked.

"I expect it's mostly a lot of speaking in soothing tones." Dad laughed. "We're hoping to pick up bottled water and some food and reduce our diner meals a bit," Dad said. "It's getting expensive."

"Bad for his waistline," I heard Mom interject.

"The shop is making lots of money, Dad." I couldn't help telling him. "It's pretty unbelievable."

"That's great. But how much are you boys working? The shop's important, but don't let it tie you down too hard," Dad said. "It's also summertime, Dewey. You need to have some fun."

Vince overheard. He grinned at me, sprung up on his toes, and pretended to cast a fishing line.

"People really need us, Dad."

"They need to chew on our butts," Vince mumbled, and I steered away from him with the phone.

Dad asked, "Are you making it to the bank with the cash? You're not leaving it all in the tin every night, are you?"

"N-no." It was a half-lie. "I'm just leaving enough to make change." I tried to think then. I might have skipped a night. Or was it two?

Vince put his face in mine again. He looked at me with one eye closed, one eye wide open. I turned my back and changed the subject with Dad.

"Dad, about the aid truck . . . well, it means there is fuel *somewhere*. Right?"

"Well, 'government reserve' or something like that. And it's making people a little crazy. They arrested a fella up here for siphoning from an aid truck in the middle of the night!" Dad said.

"Stealing gas," I mumbled. "What next?"

"Anything valuable is subject to theft," Dad said. "And values are changing out there."

As soon as I passed the phone to Lil, I grabbed the key to the shop and headed toward the door.

"Where ya goin', Dewey?" Vince gave me a smirk. He knew, and I knew, that I was going to the barn. I had a wad of cash to bring in.

16

VINCE CAME BACK FROM THE MORNING SEA Camp delivery whistling. He bounced right out to the paddock and picked up the difficult job he'd been working on the day before. No swearing.

Meanwhile, I'd taken my triage theory in a little different direction. I gave Vince the harder jobs (without mentioning to him that I knew he was the better mechanic). I knocked off the standard stuff more quickly by lining up the similar jobs and getting on a roll. I also got into the shop right after morning chores—no Angus-and-Eva drop-off. Vince did better focusing on the couple of jobs a day. And I didn't feel like a tyrant.

Well, except for the times I nagged him about the parts. True, we had a very loose system for keeping track—maybe no system at all. We'd never really needed one. But now that we were busy, I was trying to stay on top of it. Vince seemed to have no idea what he used.

I'd stand there looking at the shelves and ask him, "How many brake assemblies did you go through yesterday?" Or, "Wasn't there another roll of Teflon cable? Did you take a box of twenty-seven-inch tubes outside?"

For the first time in his life he couldn't come up with a short answer. He barely answered at all. He'd say, "No. Uh, no. I don't *think* I used that." But he sounded more like he was asking a question.

I had no time to go back through orders checking and rechecking. Not with so many repairs still waiting. My strategy was to go forward—with my brother Vince, the spaced-out bike-mechanic genius.

I kept telling myself it was okay. I was getting an earlier start now, and I was even setting myself up with the parts the night before.

Who's the genius?

"In the zone," I said to myself. I fired up the

compressor and hissed air into three tires in a row. "Oh yeah!"

Suddenly Lil was at my elbow.

"What?" I said.

And don't bother me about the shop being too full of bikes when we're having a good morning here and I'm perfectly in charge . . .

"I want that," she said. She pointed to the compressor and gave me an only slightly apologetic look.

"Don't let her have it!" Vince warned from the paddock door. "She'll flatten it with the sledge and glue it to the barn." He had a point. Lil thought everything on the planet had something to do with her art. Things went missing, then turned up sort of *re-created*.

"Back! Back!" I said, and I aimed the air hose at her.

"*Puh-leese!* I've started lots of detail work and I want to see if I can throw a lot of paint at the barn all at once," she said. "But I also need to be able to *aim*. And Dad said this would work, and I found the paint-sprayer attachment. . . ." She paused and showed it to me. "I just need today to learn how to use it and then maybe a day or two more. Can't you manage without it?"

"Ye-sss," I said. I flipped the hose out of my fingers.

So there went the compressor on its cart, rolling out the door.

Vince and I listened to Lil run it off and on for the next hour or so. Tough as she is about most things, Lil admits to being "shy of machines." There were a lot of stops and starts. In between, we could hear paint hitting the side of the barn.

I stopped Vince as he came through the shop on his way out to pick up Angus and Eva. "Does it sound like she has that pressure set kind of high?" I asked.

"Like artillery," Vince said. King of the short answer.

He might have been gone ten minutes when I heard a sudden loud *pop* and a yelp. I dropped my work and ran around to the back. The dogs galloped beside me.

The first thing I saw was the greasy blue paint

shining on the side of the barn. Test splotches, I thought. Then I saw Lil. She was blue. Painted blue. Mostly down one arm and leg. A piece of wood she was holding was also partly blue. She was otherwise all right. She stood there looking at me with her eyes wide.

"Oh! Dewey! Did you see that? W-what did it do?"

I shook my head. I looked at the compressor and the sprayer head. Then I looked at Lil. Then I knew.

"It *painted* you," I blurted. I started laughing. Hard. I could barely speak. "The compressor holds a reserve even after you shut it down. There's pressure in there, Lil! Did you have the sprayer propped on the fence post?"

She nodded.

"Well, it's on the ground now. It must have landed on its trigger."

"Oh, my heck. What are the chances . . ." She looked down the length of her arm then up at me again.

"Nice color!" I cheered.

"This," she said, "is pretty permanent stuff."

I laughed again. "At least it didn't get you in the face," I said, and I brought her a rag from her bucket. "Hey, check out your stunt double," I said. I pointed to her headless silhouette on the barn. It was a pretty clean image. The plywood scrap in her hand made it look like she was holding a book out to an invisible someone.

Lil drew a big breath. "Oh. Yes! Yes! Good little scary machine," Lil said, and she ran up to the compressor and gave it a pat. "See?" she said, looking back at the side of the barn. "It's perfect! Just what I wanted."

"You wanted to stencil yourself onto the barn?" I asked.

"Well, not *me*. But—"

I made wide eyes and stared back at her for a few seconds. "Goodie, Greatie!" I called. "Run for your lives!"

Eva cried harder. Vince shook his head at me. Angus looked at me with huge, wide eyes. "Our bikes got stole," he said.

"Somebody *stole* your bikes? Both of them? You're kidding." I looked at Vince. "For real?"

"Gone," he said. "They left the helmets. That's it." He let the bike slide to the ground.

Eva sobbed. "And my arms and legs have knots in them," she said.

Vince collapsed flat on his back. He rubbed his bicep and elbow, then stretched the arm up over his head. "Me too, Eva," he said. "I got knots too."

"Angus? You okay, buddy?" I asked.

"I'm okay, except my butt is asleep." He squeezed his cheeks and picked a wedgie. "But I helped. I held on to Eva's feet," he said.

"Yes, I saw you," I said. "You were awesome." I tried to think what Mom and Dad would say to them if they were here. Eva looked up at me.

"Nobody ever stole our bikes before!" she said. She made hiccupping sounds then erupted

17

LIL KEPT EXPERIMENTING. I KEPT WORKING. I was wheeling finished bikes out to the front for pickup like nobody's business. For the first time in days, the spindle where we'd stuck all the quick-fix jobs was clear. I did a victory dance all the way to the house. I poured a cold drink of water and wet my head under the faucet. I made a bunch of come-and-get-it phone calls to customers. Back in the barn, I picked an order from the Parts or Problems spindle. These were usually Vince's jobs. "And where in the heck is he anyway?" I mumbled. He'd been gone for over an hour. It just didn't take that long to fetch Angus and Eva.

Suddenly, I was ticked off. I'd bent over

backward to make the bike shop bearable. Mostly by getting him out a lot. I missed my morning rides to Sea Camp. Well, maybe I didn't miss the slowpoke rides there. But I sure as heck missed the all-out sprints back home.

Vince would *never* forget our twins. But he could easily lose track of time afterward. He was probably soaking up some sun. Playing on the beach with Angus and Eva. Or just freewheeling his way home with them so as to avoid work.

"Vince, you snake," I said. And then, because timing is everything, I heard a chain slipping a gear. Greatness stood up and Goodness followed. Somebody was coming down the path between the yards.

I stepped out of the barn. It was Vince. No doubt about that. He was pedaling. Strangely. He was holding Eva on his lap, huggy-bear style. He had one arm wrapped around her. He steered the bike with his other hand. Eva bumped from side to side over his knees. As they came along, I could see Angus sitting on the rear rack, backward, his heels propped up on the edge. He held Eva's feet,

one wedged under each of his arms. His eyes were closed with the effort of holding on.

"Vince!" I yelled. "What are you doing?" I jogged toward them.

"Doing—the best I can," Vince strained. "Little help?" He let the bike coast into the yard. His fingers looked stiff as he stretched them to squeeze the brake. I met him and caught the handlebars. Vince was out of breath. He stood on tiptoe balancing the bike while Eva cried, almost silently, into his chest.

"Is she hurt?" I asked.

Vince shook his head no. "I've got the bike," he said. "Get Angus down. Please."

I swept Angus from the back of the bike and let him down to the grass. Then I reached for Eva. She unpeeled slowly from Vince's chest then hung limp in my arms. "Put her down," Vince said. "She's tired. Her grip is all gone."

I sat in the grass and cradled my little sister between my knees. I carefully unbuckled her helmet. "What happened to you guys? Where are your bikes?" I asked.

again. "I was right down at the beach! I-I didn't see a robber."

I looked at Vince. "Where did you leave the bikes this morning?"

"At the side of the pavilion," he said.

"So just like always?" I said.

"Yeah," said Vince. "Only things are no longer *just like always*."

Lil came around to the yard. We gave her the bad news. "Oh! Horrible!" she said. "*Horrible!* Who could be so low as to—"

"Hey, Lil." I showed her my palm, tried to get her to back off. It just didn't seem like it was going to help to have the big sister all upset too. Lil knelt down in front of Eva.

"And you had to ride three of you to one bike? The whole way home?" She wiped Eva's cheeks with her thumbs.

"We're all in cramps," Vince said. He pulled one leg behind him to stretch his thigh.

"Vince, you could have called us," Lil said.

"Yep. My fault."

"No, I don't mean it like that." She reached

and tagged his shoulder apologetically.

"But I forgot the phone. Mattie called the police as soon as we found out the bikes were missing. But it took them forever to show up."

We could have guessed that part. We knew that most of the force were on bikes or electric carts these days. I knew of only one department wheelie pod. Besides, a pair of stolen junior bikes was hardly a high priority.

Vince went on. "Pop was out on the boat. Mattie still had afternoon campers."

"And we wanted to come home *now*," Eva spoke up.

"Sea Camp is *bad*." Angus shook his head.

"No, no, no!" Lil reached for Angus. "Sea Camp is *not* bad! Oh, Angus, baby, please don't say that!" Lil grabbed him up, hugging him hard. "Our Mattie is there! You have a good time with her."

"Our bikes got stole," he said again. He twisted his face up—ugliest look I'd ever seen on my little brother. Lil tucked his head under her chin and rocked him.

"I didn't know it'd be so hard to carry two," Vince said.

"You did a great job," Lil said. "Everyone did a great job."

We were all quiet for a few minutes. Then Angus said, "Lil?"

"Yes?"

"Why do you have blue on you?" He patted her painted hand.

"Oh!" Lil laughed. "By mistake! I accidentally spray-painted myself."

"I like it," said Eva.

"Yeah, me too," said Angus.

"Thank you," said Lil.

"Can I get blue too?"

"Well . . . *maybe*," Lil said. "Here's what I was thinking . . ." She began to talk about her mural. "I keep thinking about the gas being all gone," she began, "and it makes me wish we all could fly . . . just spread our arms like birds and go up."

"I wish Mom and Dad could," said Eva.

"I wish I could," said Angus. "Because if I had

111

wings I wouldn't take them off. Then they couldn't get stole."

We were still sitting on the grass when Runks and Macey came up on their copsicles.

"Hello, Marrisses!" Runks called. "So sorry, all! So sorry about the missing mini Marriss bikes. We heard about it from dispatch."

"Oh, thanks for stopping," Lil said.

Officer Macey hopped off his copsicle. "Couldn't believe it when I found out it was you guys," he said. "Hey, look what I brought." He stooped down and offered two lollipops to our tear-stained twins. "Come on now. Gotta cheer up. Huh?"

"So, I suppose you'll let us know if you hear anything or find anything? About the bikes?" Lil said. But she didn't sound hopeful.

Runks nodded. "It'll be difficult," he admitted. To me, that meant we had little chance of getting them back.

"I'll put some extra time on it when I can," Macey said.

"Well, that's nice, but I'm sure you have bigger

problems out there these days," Lil said.

For some reason that made me think about the day I'd picked her up on the highway—how she'd said, *Weird times, civilian rule.* Just how big was that? What would I do if I came upon those two small bikes somewhere? Would I take them back? Would that be stealing from two more little kids, or would I be reclaiming something for my family? For Angus and Eva? Questions without answers.

"I'd like to see those bikes returned," Macey said.

I turned to the twins. "Vince and I will start collecting parts to build two new bikes for you guys."

"Absolutely," said Vince.

"It'll take a while. But we'll do it. I promise," I said.

"I wish it could be my real bike," said Angus. "And I just wish it was time for Mom and Dad to call."

Pop and Mattie showed up while the officers were still with us. I was glad to have everyone around, but Lil seemed bothered. "Oh, my gosh.

Hey, everybody. Not to worry. We're all right. Really. We're even lucky enough to have a carrier these guys can ride in."

"I just feel so bad," Mattie said. "My campers have always left their bikes by the pavilion and they've never locked them up. Never!"

I remembered how Dad had said anything valuable is subject to theft. But stealing junior bikes seemed especially mean somehow.

"It's happening everywhere," Runks said, and he shook his head.

Pop and Mattie had brought scallops and crabmeat, and they wanted to stay and have dinner together. Lil spoke up again. "Oh, you don't have to feed us," she told them. "We're fine, fine, fine!"

"Are you sure?" said Pop. "Because you're looking a bit blue." He grinned and grabbed her painted hand and shook it. He leaned toward her and begged, "Please don't make me bike that seafood back home." Lil finally gave up a small grin, and I knew they'd be staying.

Before he left, Macey repeated that he'd keep looking into the case of the twin's bikes himself. It was nice to think that it mattered to him.

Dinner was a little quiet right up until I suddenly caught sight of Mr. Spivey coming around the fence. He was leading Gloria Cloud through the gate and into our paddock.

"What?" I gasped. I whispered to Lil. "Did you loan Gloria Cloud to the Spive today?"

"No. Why?"

I pointed. "He must have helped himself," I said.

"To your sheep? Aw! The nerve!" Pop banged his hand on the table. "I say, *the nerve*!"

"But wait!" said Lil. "He's making a little history here."

"What? Overcoming his dread of droppings?" Vince said.

"No. He's bringing her *back*! Without bothering us," Lil said. "I'm telling you, this is *history*!"

"I don't know," said Pop. "He took her in the first place. Could be time for that geezer-to-geezer chat."

Lil rolled her eyes. "Pop, don't worry. We're *so* used to him."

"Yep. Used to him like a tack stuck in your toe," Pop said. "Egg thief. Berry snatcher." The twins giggled, and Pop got louder. "*Zu*-cchini robber. *Sheep bandit!*"

"Shh! Pop!" Mattie gave him an elbow and quite a look. "The Marrisses have an understanding with their neighbor. All is well."

"I'll tell you what is well. Their neighbor is *well fed*, and his *lawn* is well trimmed, all thanks to the Marrisses."

Lil rose from the picnic table. "Well, Pop, we're well fed tonight because of you. Thank you for the scallops and the crab, too."

"Pop always brings a little bit of *crab*," Mattie said. Pop could not help laughing at that.

That night, while Angus and Eva soaped dishes at the sink, I swept the floors. Lil had sent the dogs upstairs to "beg from above," which meant they hung out on the balcony just above the kitchen table with their noses between the rails. Vince made a game of jumping up and trying to set dog treats under their noses. The danger was overfeeding. Old Goodness was a bit of a puker. But at least Vince's athletics made us laugh and cheer a few times. Then Lil took the call from Mom and Dad.

"It hasn't been the best day," I heard her say. "But we're all right."

Apparently the first thing Mom and Dad did was ask Lil to please say those two sentences in the *reverse* order in the future. She'd given them both minor heart attacks.

"I'm going to let Angus tell you," she said. She let him dry his hands then gave him the phone. Eva closed in to listen with him. We could have delivered the next lines in unison.

"Mom. Dad. Our bikes got stole."

I didn't hear exactly what Mom and Dad said, but the rhythm of their voices seemed consoling. The twins kept nodding as they held the receiver between them. Then Eva suddenly said, "We are going back to Sea Camp tomorrow. Because we want to *make history*."

I looked at Lil. She scrunched up her face. Vince had an ear on the conversation too.

"Like Mr. Spivey," Eva went on. "He made

history today. He stole Gloria Cloud. But then he brought her back when he was done with her. So the robber guys could put our bikes back at the pavilion. When they're done with them."

Lil, Vince, and I had a collective heart dive.

While Lil helped Angus and Eva get ready for bed, she explained to them that it was not likely that the bikes would be returned to Sea Camp.

"That's what Mom said too," Eva said. "But I'm making a wish."

Later on, when our twins had fallen asleep, Lil asked, "Do you guys have any little bike frames in the shop?"

"Sixteen inchers? Not a one." I shook my head and let out a sigh.

18

"PSST! DEWEY. I NEED YOU TO GET UP." LIL SHOOK my arm. I sat up in the attic bedroom and looked over at Vince. Unconscious.

"D-did I oversleep? Do I have customers?" I squinted at the clock.

"No, but heads-up. Change of plan." She looked stern.

Lil . . . taking charge. Of something. Now if only I could wake up . . .

"I need you guys to meet me at Shoreland's Market right after you drop off Angus and Eva. I've been watching the news. Trucks still aren't moving. I did a cupboard check. I don't like it. We need to get there this morning."

I whispered. "Are you kidding? Lil, I *have* to

get into the shop. Vince does the camp drop now. Take him." I jabbed a thumb toward my sleeping brother.

"Yeah, right. Vince in the grocery store?" Lil whispered.

She was right. Vince was a notoriously terrible shopper. He tried to follow the list, but he'd get off track and start picking up whatever. Then he'd come home embarrassed and bewildered by what was in the grocery sacks. And what wasn't.

"I'm going to have Vince babysit the bikes while you and I shop," Lil said. "Last thing we need is another theft. You and Vince put the carrier on the tandem. Haul Angus and Eva to camp. Meet me, and then we'll fill it with groceries for the way home. I've got the panniers and we'll all bring backpacks," Lil said. "Oh, and you have money, right?"

Ah. Now she would understand about all those bikes in the shop. I reached below my bed and dragged out one of my work boots. I pulled a roll of bills out of it and thunked it into her hand.

"Cripes! Dewey!" she squawked. That made

Vince sit up. "Ever heard of making a deposit? How much is here?" She sniffed the wad. Must have been the smell of peppermint. Not essence of work boot.

"A lot," I said. "B-but it's just because I held on to a bunch for the trip to Bocci. And Robert Deal paid cash for his bike."

"Negligent." Vince yawned and fell back on his pillow.

Lil wasn't amused. "Unreal, Dewey. Staying on top of the banking is part of taking care of the Bike Barn. Dad would worry if he knew!"

I felt my face flush. "Yeah, well, who was supposed to stay on top of the groceries?" I felt bad as soon as I said it and worse when I saw Lil's face pink up too.

She flipped through the bills instead of looking at me. "Well, I guess we've both been crunched, then," she said. "We'll have to do better. Meet me at Shoreland's." She gave my bed a hard bounce as she got up.

I yawned and said, "It's a plan."

19

SHORELAND'S MARKET WAS PACKED. I FOUND LIL in the produce section. She was holding a grape in her finger and thumb. I faked a gasp.

"Did you *pick* that?" I asked. (Time to make nice with her.) "You renegade. You deviant. Picking and eating in the grocery store." I shook my head. (Had to have some fun. I *belonged* in the Bike Barn.)

Lil wrinkled her nose at me and said, "First, I wouldn't eat *this* if you paid me. Second, I did *not* pick it. I didn't have to. They're falling off the vines. And they're all spongy." She set the grape back into one of the bunches and several more rolled off the vine. "None of this produce looks good," she said. "And look, no lemons."

"Maybe Mrs. Bertalli will visit again."

"Well, it's not like we *need* lemons." Lil looked around at the produce section once more. "We have fresh stuff in the garden. Dark greens are full of C, right? And the early tomatoes, too. So we're not going to end up with scurvy just yet. Let's skip this and move on."

She steered our cart around the cheese case, which wasn't full but wasn't empty, either. I picked up a small wheel of cheddar and pressed it over my head a few times. "What do you say?" I asked.

Lil checked the sticker. "Hmm . . . yeah, let's do it. It's not cheap, but I can see us carving off of that for a while." I rolled the cheese wheel off my hand and into our cart.

"Okay, what's next?" I said.

The shelves in Shoreland's were spotty in places and completely empty in others. I wondered how the big chain stores were doing. Shoreland's bought a lot of locally grown and produced foods, and I thought maybe they were better off during the crunch.

"This is so surreal," Lil breathed. She pushed the cart slowly. "Look at these shelves." She rested her chin on her knuckles. "The empty spaces."

I went up behind her, cupped my mouth with my hands, and called, "Black hole in aisle two. Black hole in aisle two."

She swatted at me like the fly that I was. Then she was quiet for a few seconds. She stood staring at the shelves, then at other people's carts. The look on her face was suddenly strange. "I think we should skip the list and just get what we can get," she said. "And a lot of it."

"What do you mean?"

"Let's just get to it," she said. She leaned toward me and spoke quietly. "Start picking things that we can store for a while. Like that cheddar. That was a good one, Dew."

Now I was kind of creeped out. This grocery run felt like a preemptive strike. We got oats and brown rice. I picked up two bags of quinoa, because Mom called it "God's greatest grain that nobody is eating." We got a hard salami, summer sausages, and ten cans each of sardines and tuna fish. We loaded our cart with bags of beans and boxes of pasta. Then, because we had no choice, and because we love our dogs, we slid a big bag of chow onto the bottom of the cart. That was going to take up a lot of space in the bike carrier, I thought.

At the checkout, Lil suddenly went jogging back through the store in search of dried fruit. She came back—grinning just a little, finally—with a tall round box of raisins and a tray of dried apricots.

Outside Shoreland's Market, we met Vince, who'd been snoozing in the sun next to our bikes. We set to loading up. The carrier filled quickly. We tucked cans and packages all around the dog chow. The panniers sagged, but we made them sag evenly.

"Nothing lighter than a brick for sale, I see," Vince said.

"I know. These cans, the cheese. Bags of grains. What were we thinking?" I said.

Lil took my question seriously. "We were thinking that the trucks still aren't rolling," she said. I waited a beat.

"You really think this is going to last longer, don't you? You think that Mom and Dad are still days out, don't you?" There. I had said it.

Lil shrugged. Suddenly, I wanted to know *how* long it'd be. And if the answer was a month, well, okay. I just wanted to know the plan.

"I think—I have no idea what to think," Lil said. "But a lot of people are going to start . . . well . . . they're going to start doing what we're doing," she said. She gestured toward our packages of food.

"Do you think we're hoarding?" I asked. Lil didn't answer me right away. She muscled her way into the straps of her stuffed backpack and tightened up on the waist belt.

"I guess you could call it that," Lil said. "Or you could say that I don't want Pop and Mattie or anyone else thinking they have to come feed us every night. But most of all, I'm making sure that I never have to tell Angus and Eva that there's no supper."

We pedaled our weighed-down bikes toward home. The tandem frame complained beneath Vince and me every so often.

"Dew, let's bike out," Vince said, and I felt him push his pedal set. We could have gone faster. But I didn't want to leave Lil behind. I turned my head back to tell him no.

At home, I brought the big bag of dog food in

on my shoulder and let it down to the floor. The dogs came over, wiggling and wagging, as if to say, "Yeah, yeah! This is ours!" That made Lil laugh. Then the Athletes strutted in through the open door. Chickens in the house are always funny. But I think it was looking at a full pantry that really lightened Lil's mood.

When I carried the cheese and sausages down to the cellar, I took a quick look at what was left from last year's canning. There were still a few jars each of tomatoes, peaches, some pickled beans. We had food ripening in the garden. I got a funky feeling in my gut. That suddenly seemed both good and bad. Canning season was coming again. But surely Mom and Dad would be home by then. They *had* to be.

Back upstairs, Lil was almost done filling all our big jars with oats and rice. Vince had filled the dog-food bin.

"You guys can go," Lil said. "But take the animals with you."

I clapped my hands in the air and called the dogs. Vince and I each pinned a chicken in our hands and headed out the door.

20

FOR THE FIRST TIME EVER, TWO BIKES HAD BEEN left off while we were gone. I had to laugh. One person had scribbled us a note. The other person must not have had paper with him because he'd used the back of the first guy's note to leave his information.

Vince went into the shop ahead of me and opened up the door to his paddock. I stood still for a moment and took in the smell of the grease and rubber, the wooden walls. So much work waited, so many bikes, and two more to log in. So how could it be that I thought of this shop as my oasis? But it *was* my oasis—from the upside-down world of empty fuel tanks and useless ration cards, bike thieves at the beaches and barren shelves at Shoreland's Market—

"Ah, good. You're finally here!"

I snapped around and found myself face-to-face with Mr. Gilmartin, who seemed to be burning a hole through my forehead with his stare. Time warped. I registered Lil, passing behind him on her way out to her mural. Her oasis, I thought.

"This is my second time by this morning," Mr. Gilmartin said.

"Good morning," I said.

He nodded. Seemed pleasant. Not angry. "I've changed my mind about the derailleur," he said. "I think you were right. This one is back to rough shifting—not that I blame you. I can see you did what you could. But it's driving me nuts. I'm on the bike at least two hours a day now. I want to go with that upgrade," he said. "Why not? I've spent a whole lot more to improve the performance of my car in the past."

"I'll show you what the part will cost," I said, sticking to the facts right from the get-go. I put the invoice that Mr. Bocci had given me right under Mr. Gilmartin's nose. "Here is what I paid. That's what you pay," I said. "Labor by the hour."

"Yes." He was not thrilled. "But you have it in stock?"

I turned to the bench and pulled the box out. It was the only high-end derailleur I had—the best one for Gilmartin's bike. It was also one of the items I had hesitated to take from Mr. Bocci. But now, just maybe everything was turning out all right. I lifted the lid and showed him the part. It was beautiful—forged aluminum, carbon fiber.

"Then let's do it," he said.

"Okay, I'll log you in."

"Log me in?" Gilmartin's face contorted. "No, no. I've already waited once. And you know that."
Here we go again.

Vince stepped inside from the paddock. He fiddled with something over on the bench, then stood by. I had to give my public-phobic brother credit. Even silent support took some pressure off. I drew a breath.

"Mr. Gilmartin, we appreciate your business. But everyone feels like you feel. Everyone needs their bikes back ASAP."

"But I *assumed* you'd put me through," he snapped. When I didn't budge, he huffed in disbelief. Then he started to get loud. "Look, I paid your *sky-high* price before, and I'm willing to pay this now. But I don't want to wait a second time!" Now he was yelling.

"We share your frustration with the high prices, sir," I said. (What a great phrase, I thought. I hoped I could remember that one if I ever needed it again.) Meanwhile, Vince shifted next to me. "But putting this job ahead of others—well, it wouldn't be fair to the people who have been waiting."

"So you're going to put me back at the end of the line to address the *same area* of my bike again?"

"Y-yes. If you'd been *dissatisfied* with our work, I—"

"I am dissatisfied with your *bad business practice*!" he yelled.

Now I could hear my heart in my ears. Heck, I could hear Vince's heart in my ears.

Gilmartin went on. "Then again, what did I *expect* from a *rinky-dink* operation?" He scoffed and flung the back of his hand toward our work-bench. "Nothing but a bunch of *coffee canners!*"

"'Coffee canners'?" I said.

Vince gave me some wide eyeballs. He pointed a finger at our peppermint tin but hid the gesture from Gilmartin.

Suddenly, I was fuming. Who was this guy to insult us for not having a cash register? And calling us *rinky-dink*?

Don't break. Stick to facts, I told myself.

"Mr. Gilmartin, please don't make me *refuse* to serve you," I said. I let a second go by—waited in the warm Bike Barn air. Then I told him, "The way I see it, there's only one question: Do you want this new derailleur or not?"

So strange—my heart actually quieted down then. I looked at my feet. I listened to the fan. I smelled the aroma of my oasis. I longed to turn my back on Gilmartin and start the next job on my spindle. But I needed his answer even more.

"Have you decided?" I asked.

His skin was red all up his neck, his lips in a straight line. Finally, he nodded. "I'd like to have you install the new derailleur," he said.

Then I heard somebody say, "O-okay." It was Vince! He spoke! He even passed me an order slip and a pen.

As I wrote, I told Gilmartin, "Please know that we *want* to get your bike back to you as fast as we can." Nothing could have been truer.

Mr. Gilmartin finally walked out of the shop. I set the derailleur in its box and slid it to the back of the workbench.

A minute or so later, Vince piped up. "That guy's a gripe-a-pottamus," he said, as if he'd just figured that out.

"Yeah. He's kind of like the Spive," I said. "What is it Mom says? He's 'invested in being unhappy'? Something like that?"

21

IT WAS SIX O'CLOCK WHEN VINCE AND I degreased, washed up, and met Lil and the twins at the picnic table. That's when we realized that though we had food, we had no dinner plan.

"Ack!" Lil said. "I was lost in it out there this afternoon. It was great!" She smiled. "When the work is a winner—"

"—you forget to eat dinner!" Angus and Eva finished her rhyme.

"Well, what do we want? Who has an idea?"

We heard a cluck or two, and one of the Athletes jumped onto the table. The bird shook herself. A puff of dust settled below her.

"We're *not* going to eat you," Angus said, and he lifted the hen down. The hen's chicken feet were stenciled in the dust.

Lil stared at the prints with a slight grin on her face. "Look at that. Cool," she said. Then getting back to the matter at hand, she said, "Well, we always have eggs."

We all heard someone call out. "Am I too late for dinner?"

Timing is everything.

Robert Deal came riding into our yard. The first thing I noticed was a new headlight on his bike. The second was the pizza box—make that *three* pizza boxes—bungeed to the back rack of his bike.

"Hey, Robert!" I called. "How's the bike?"

"I *love* this bike," he said. "I love it so much I brought you all a thank-you dinner. No anchovies!" He greeted our dogs first, then he untied the boxes and set them on our table.

"Pizza!" cried Eva. "Angus, don't you love pizza more than eggs?"

"Yeah. I do."

"Wait, wait. You brought us dinner?" Lil said. "You didn't have to—"

"*Thanks!*" I said. I was freakishly loud. I didn't

want Lil to have a chance to go into her we're-fine-on-our-own mode. Something smelled seriously good—better than eggs—and I didn't want it leaving the yard.

"You guys ever go to the Old Stone Oven in East Elm City?" Robert asked. "Best pizza I know of. And they're still up and running."

Vince sighed. "Oh. Ye-s-s."

"And you biked it all the way here?" Lil said.

"Yeah. I tried not to sway," he said. "It's probably still hot because, well, what isn't hot today?" He threw open the boxes on the picnic table and I think Lil understood there'd be no turning down this gift.

Robert gave us the latest news from the open road while we ate. He'd seen two government-aid trucks posted along the highway.

"Oh, Mom and Dad said the same," I told Robert. "There is fuel somewhere."

"Genius," Vince said.

"I just really want Mom and Dad to get that tank filled up." Eva leaned on her elbows and pouted. Robert slid a piece of pizza under her nose, and she snapped right out of her funk.

"I was thinking about them," Robert said. "What's the news?"

"They're still stuck. Can't really get Mom south to the trains, and even if they could, it doesn't seem to be a sure thing. So they're still waiting it out."

"And staying together," Lil added.

"Man, I'm sorry."

"But we're fine," Lil said. "We are *so* used to this. There's nothing Mom and Dad can do for us that we can't do for ourselves." I wasn't so sure that was true. But I knew she was trying to hammer home a message to Robert: *We don't need help.*

"Yes. You seem very self-sufficient," he said.

I drifted then. Took a look around our property—the part I could see from where I sat. Raspberries were popping off the vines along the fence next to Mr. Spivey's house. In fact, we were wasting them. Mom wasn't here to make jam. None of us had taken the time to pick them—except for Mr. Spivey, who happened to be stealing from us through the slats of the fence at that very moment. The canes bobbed as he nabbed handfuls of fruit.

What's a few berries between neighbors? I could almost hear Dad say.

Lil gave me a poke in the arm. "Where are you, Dew?"

"Oh. Spacing out," I said.

"Hey, that's my job," said Vince, and everyone laughed.

I left my real thought behind. "I was just thinking," I said, "that we should pick raspberries for dessert."

There was a rustling sound just over the fence. Then Mr. Spivey's screen door slammed shut.

Soon Robert Deal was lifting Angus up so he could reach the highest raspberry canes. Later, he put the leftover pizza in our fridge for us and folded the box down into the fire pit. He had an easy way about him. Mom would have said he was a "comfortable sort."

Lil wanted to trace outlines of the twins on brown paper that night. It had something to do with her mural, but I was just glad it would entertain the twins. She said she'd run them a shower afterward.

I wanted to clean up the shop a bit, dust being the enemy of all things with moving parts.

Robert came to the Bike Barn with Vince and me, and the dogs, of course. "Doesn't look like things have slowed down any in here," he said.

"Buried in bikes," said Vince.

"Well, actually we cleared a bunch today," I said. "But then we took in a bunch more."

"Oh, and you stocked up on parts. That was smart."

I told him about my trip to Bocci Bike. He told me they'd sold him the new headlight and had admired his Marriss-built bike. I made a note to tell Dad about that.

Robert seemed to like being in the shop. Of course, he spent a while just patting our dogs. But then he helped us straighten up. He even ran the Shop-Vac for us. Vince and I moved away from the noise and stood out in the paddock under the yellow lamp and sorted the next day's orders.

Robert helped us lay out parts with order slips for upcoming jobs. (It was my latest method for getting a jump on things every day.) He seemed truly interested in bikes. He stood reading Dad's One-Page Bible for Bike Mechanics and followed it up with a slow-breaking grin. "This is great," he said, tapping a finger on the paper. "Eight rules, and they all make sense."

"That's how we learned," I said.

"And we used cheat sheets," Vince said.

Robert laughed. "Like there's a way to *cheat* at bike repairs!"

"Sort of," I said. I opened the bench drawer, reached inside, and pulled out a few three-by-five cards. "Our dad made these up for us for the most common repair jobs." I flipped through them. "You'll have to meet our dad someday," I said. "When the crunch is over."

Together, the three of us slid the big door shut and locked up the shop. We thanked Robert for the pizza supper and the leftovers. (I knew what I was having for breakfast.) He suddenly remembered and gave us back the flashlight I'd lent him.

I felt bad about just one thing after he left. I hadn't asked him how his job hunt was going. But by the next morning, I knew.

22

"HEY, DEWEY." ROBERT DEAL STOOD AT THE OPEN Bike Barn door. The morning sun wasn't quite over the trees. Vince was taking Angus and Eva to camp. Lil was—where else?—out back of the barn.

"Oh, hey, Robert!" I said. Then I worried. Why was he here? "Oh my gosh, did something happen to your bike?"

"No. The bike is fine. I'm not even sure why I'm here," he said, and laughed. "Dewey, I don't know if you can understand this, but I am a *displaced person*. I *need* to work. I *like* to work. I started out on the highway again this morning on the old job hunt. But the truth is, there's nothing left for me to look at right now. I'm okay for money for a while.

So . . . would you mind if I hung around your shop today? I'll—I'll try to help. I'll at least stay out of the way. I'm sort of mechanically inclined, and—"

"Be my guest!" I said. "Where do you want to start?"

"Hey, that's up to you, Boss Man. I'm the drone."

"Well, here. Disassemble this bearing set," I said. I handed him a cone wrench. "The proper tool for the job," I said. "It's Rule Two." I tapped Dad's list with my knuckles. "There might even be a cheat sheet in the drawer. But basically, get it apart without undue force. Then put the parts in the degreasing bath one at a time as you separate them."

"Okay," said Robert.

"When they're clean, lay them out on the toweling in the same order they came apart. That's part of Rule Five. Study the problem. Seeing how it works helps. Trust me. And if you have questions, just ask me."

"Or me!" said Vince as he came through the

door. "Hi, Robert. You hanging around today?"

"Yeah," said Robert. "I've always liked taking stuff apart. I was thinking you guys could teach me how to put something together again."

"Cool. An *apprentice*," Vince said. "Looks just like a *willing victim*." He slinked out to the paddock.

I followed him out. "Hey, Vince. Did you bring a spoke wrench out here?" I did a quick search of the grass for anything shiny.

"Nope. I haven't trued up a wheel in days. That's you," he said, and for once he seemed very sure.

"Hmm. Well, did you use that fifteen-speed gear set? We had one set out last night."

Vince shook his head. "No. I didn't do that job. You always think it's *me* when you can't find something." He stood up with his arms wide. Gave me a sideways grin. "Wanna have me X-rayed?"

"No. Forget it," I said. I scanned the paddock one last time. I had no time to hunt. We owned half a dozen spoke wrenches and I had a couple of more gear sets on the shelf inside. Maybe I was wrong.

Maybe I hadn't set it aside. Maybe it'd turn up later.

Through the morning, we could hear Lil banging on the barn. I knew she'd cut out a bunch of paper tracings last night—Angus's and Eva's—all in different flying positions. There had been a mad search for a staple gun early that morning. She had to be tacking them up now. Maybe she would spray today and be done with my compressor. Every so often I'd hear the scaffold thump on the barn wall. It was a heavy old thing and it had to be all she could do to move it by herself. But would Lilly Marriss ask for help? No.

Vince left to pick up Angus and Eva, and Robert and I went to the house for lunch and iced tea. Lil came running in, calling my name.

"Dewey! Hey, hey! Dewey!" She stopped in her tracks when she saw us. "Oh. Robert," she said, and with each word her face seemed to drop a little more. "You're here again."

"Hi, Lilly. How's it going?" Robert said.

"Okay. Fine," she said. I pushed a glass of tea her way and she took it. "So what brings you back again so soon?" Lil said.

"Umm . . . umm." I tucked a bite of pizza into my cheek. "The job hunt stinks. He's hanging out with Vince and me today. He's helping. It's great!"

"I hope it's all right," Robert said, looking at Lil. "I mean, with everyone."

Lil didn't answer.

"Hey, what were you going to tell me?" I asked her.

"Oh," she said, "it was just—well, I'm getting ready to spray again."

"Cool," I said. I grinned at her. "When do I get the compressor back?"

She shook a finger at me. "We'll talk about that tonight, when we're folding laundry. And we *will* be folding laundry, Dew."

That afternoon, I barely saw Angus and Eva.

Vince checked up on them at some point and gave me the short answer. "Painting with Lil. Everyone is happy." That was good enough for me. I kept on working.

Robert was good new energy for the Bike Barn.

He had questions, so we talked, and Vince even moved his bike stand closer to the paddock door just to listen in and comment now and then. In the late afternoon, I took a quick look through the spindles. I just liked knowing what tomorrow had in store.

I mumbled as I read the names and jobs. "Fleming, brake shoes. Dominico, shifters. Gilmartin—*blech. Gilmartin.*"

Vince laughed. "Tough customer," he told Robert, and I nodded sort of absently.

I told Robert, "He called us rinky-dink coffee canners 'cause the shop's in a barn and we put the money in a tin."

"Oh, that's just rude," Robert said.

"And wrong," said Vince. "*Not* a coffee can. A peppermint tin."

Robert laughed. "And you keep milk-and-egg-money in a teapot," he said. "That makes you a teapotter, too, then." He stuck a finger at me and said, "*Teapotter.*"

We were laughing and working when Lil came up and slapped her palm on the door. "Hey, you guys," she said. The three of us looked up. The twins were right behind her. "Plan to knock off pretty soon. Vince, I want a pit fire. I'm making chili and I don't want to heat up the house. Dew, I want the clothes brought off the line. Don't miss the ones on the fence rail. We'll fold while we cook."

Being the parents, I thought.

"On it," Vince said.

"Hi, Vince! Hi, Dewey! Oh, hi, Robert Deal," Eva said. She carried a roll of brown paper against her chest. Angus had dirty paintbrushes in his hands. Rainbow-colored drips ran down his wrist. "We made our own mur-wall," Eva said.

"*Mural,*" said Lil.

"Well." Robert looked at them expectantly. "Let's see!" he said.

Angus dropped the brushes in the dirt. They spread the brown paper out and began to explain.

"We're painting Mom and Dad in the truck, right here," Angus said. "I did this part." He'd made a boxy truck with a long row of wheels underneath it.

"And over here is where they're going to get

diesel," Eva said. She pointed to a square with a long hose coming out of it. "Here is the highway, and this is our house . . ."

Robert listened to all of it, then said, "I see. It's *very* nice."

"But our sister is making a *real* mur-wall on the barn," Eva said. "And she has a scaffold and—"

"And tomorrow she's going to move it one more time and then we can climb right in the hay door! From outdoors!" Angus pointed madly. Eva jumped up and down. I thought they were both going to hyperventilate.

"Robert, are you staying for dinner?" Eva asked.

A beat went by before Lil said, "You're welcome to stay."

"Great, then!" I said. I decided to answer for him.

"Don't forget," Lil said. "The laundry and the pit. Pretty quick now."

Vince had a flame going by the time I'd cleaned up and brought the laundry basket to the picnic table. I set the mountain of clothes down gently.

Balanced it with my hands. Robert snapped a T-shirt off the top.

"No, no, no." Lil picked the shirt out of his hands. "You can't fold our laundry."

"Bet I can," he said.

Lil smiled only slightly. "But you *may not*," she said.

It turned out he might *not* chop onions, carrots, or green peppers either. I thought she was making a stupid show of the whole we-can-do-it-on-our-own thing.

Way to make the "comfortable sort" uncomfortable, Lil.

Robert didn't linger after supper. The minute he was far enough down our driveway to be out of hearing range, Lil turned to me. We were still working on the laundry. She shook a pair of my own boxers at me.

"So, Dewey, what gives with Robert being in the shop all day?"

"What do you mean?"

"Is he playing Mr. Good Samaritan here? Does he think he's rescuing us?"

"Rescuing us from what?" I said. "He's learning stuff. And he's pretty good, too."

"Look, I know you are managing the Bike Barn, but you need to talk to me about changes like that."

"Like what? Letting a guy hang around and help for the day?"

"Yes."

"Okay. Um . . . he's coming back to hang around tomorrow," I said.

Vince cracked up.

"You!" Lil pointed a finger at him. "Go get Angus and Eva started on dishes. And tell them I said not too much soap. The counter was all slippery this morning."

Vince took a stack of clean clothes into the house with him. Lil sat, giving me a piercing look from across the table.

"What?" I said.

"I'm serious," she said. "You're in charge of the shop, but don't forget I'm in charge of *everything*." She drew a wide circle in the air with a sweep of her arm. "So I can't ignore what's happening in that barn. If Robert's coming back, then let's be clear that he's *not* babysitting us, and we're *not* his community-service project. We are doing just fine." She snapped a towel out of the laundry and gave it a firm folding. "He's a bike mechanic. And you need to pay him."

I think I was probably curling a lip at her, just trying to wrap my head around all those words. I shrugged and answered, "Okay."

"Good. Next thing," she said. "All those bikes in the shop and the paddock . . . everywhere. It looks like it's gaining on you. Maybe it's time to slow it down."

I stared back at my sister. "You have got to be kidding me."

"Think about it. Vince has been stressed out—"

"He was! But I made an adjustment for that!" I stood up. "Besides, I don't *make* him work," I said. "Not ever."

"Right. But he feels like he's supposed to be there whenever you are. That's most of the time. Also, do you know what day it is, Dew?"

I probably gave her a blank look while I thought about it.

"Friday," she said. "And Sea Camp's over. Angus and Eva will be home all day from now on. I'm not doing all their care by myself."

"So! I'm ready for that," I said. (I wasn't.)

"Dewey, I think Dad is worried about you and the shop."

"He said so? To you?"

"He said it to *you*. Didn't you hear? He wants you to back off and be a kid! Have a little bit of a summer. We're going to be okay. The work will still be there when Dad gets back to help you."

"Right! So why not log it in? Most of those bikes aren't rideable anyway, Lil. People don't like the wait. But they can't walk those heaps all the way to Bocci Bike and Rec in Sand Orchard. When Dad gets back, we'll get through the orders all the faster. Besides, people count on us. Especially now. Do you have any idea how many bikes Vince and I have put back on the road since Mom and Dad left?"

"Dew, you've been awesome. But I'm supposed

to look out for you, and—"

"Look out for *me*? I don't need you looking out for me! What am I? Another five-year-old? I'm managing that shop while you're hanging off a scaffold—"

"Hey!" She stopped me cold. "Don't say it! I didn't expect to spend my summer like this— covering everything that needs to be done around here. I'm supposed to be in a class. In the city. So don't even say it, Dewey! Don't!" She pulled her lips in. She was done talking.

I was done listening. I left the laundry and stomped off into the shop. I rolled the door shut behind me and leaned on it.

Hanging off a scaffold.

Okay. Superstupid thing to say to Lil. She was right; this was not the summer of her dreams. I felt like dirt.

Only two things in this world seem to set me straight when everything else has collided. One is a long, all-out bike ride. The other is a cleaning frenzy. The way I saw it, I didn't particularly deserve the bike ride. Not until I apologized to Lil, and well, I wasn't up for the taste of crow so soon after supper. Robert had run the Shop-Vac just the night before, so not much dust was floating around. I looked at the paper slips and the parts all plunked down on the bench ready for tomorrow.

The inventory, I thought. That's sort of like cleaning.

I set to counting everything in sight. I made lists. I took a look at all the logged-in jobs and compared them to the parts we had in stock. Then I spent a while trying to stuff away the feeling that maybe Lil was right; maybe this was gaining on me—just a little bit.

23

ON SATURDAY AFTERNOON, ROBERT AND I heard lots of scrambling and rustling above the shop. He glanced up and said, "You grow big squirrels here on the Marriss mini-farm."

Then we heard a victory cheer. "We did it!" *Stomp, stomp, stomp!* Dust fell from the boards above us.

I called to Vince, "Psst! Here they come!"

Angus and Eva threw open the Trap with a bang. They appeared at the hole and called, "Who's down there?"

I answered them with a load roar and a growl. A second later Angus and Eva came running down the stairs into the shop.

"We made it!" Eva said. "All the way up the scaffold!"

"And in the hay door!" Angus shouted. "And here we go again!"

They took lap after lap. I watched them turning redder and redder in the dry heat. "They could use a run under the hose," I mumbled. "And maybe a sandwich."

"Hey, you know what?" Robert said. He set a wrench down and wiped his hands on a rag. "I say we all go for ice cream."

"Ice cream?" Vince came around the corner.

"Come on. Let's lock up. Just for an hour, Boss Man. Hallenrock Dairy is still open. Everybody should have a weekend. Or at least a couple of hours off on a Saturday." Robert gave me a convincing sort of nod.

"I'm with him." Vince pointed at Robert with a socket wrench.

"Have Angus and Eva even had lunch?" I asked Vince.

He shrugged. "They were in the garden for a while."

"Yeah, but they're not *rabbits*," I said.

"Bet they're hotter than they are hungry."

"Come on!" Robert said again. "Angus and Eva will like this."

I looked at Vince. "Okay. We'll take the tandem? We'll pull the twins together?"

"You're on," said Vince.

On their next run through the shop, I caught Angus and Eva in my monster arms and told them, "*We're* going to make *you* eat *ice cream*!" They ran squealing around the back of the barn to tell Lil.

Big surprise: She decided to go with us. (I was a little sorry. I wanted points for taking Angus and Eva off her hands for a while.)

"Dew, bring money from the tin. We'll treat at the dairy," she said.

I locked up. We loaded up. We took the path toward the shore roads, figuring we'd catch the sea breeze. On our way through the yards we saw Mr. Spivey staring at the back of the barn. As we broke through the shade, Lil said, "I don't think he loves my mural."

I said, "Well, then you're doing good work!"

We saw Officer Macey coming along Beach Road.

"Hey, Officer Plainclothes!" Lil called out. "We're heading out to Hallenrock Dairy. Want to come?"

"Wish I could," he said. "I'm on duty in less than an hour. Hallenrock is a little too far out in the wrong direction. But thanks!"

The sea breeze felt awesome—a reminder of summer beach days when I had nothing to do but push my toes into the sand and keep my lunch away from the gulls. But I could not have relaxed into a day like that. Not while I was managing the Bike Barn. As we got closer to the dairy, I got a wicked case of shop fever. Kept feeling like I ought to be working, and like Officer Macey had said, I was heading in the wrong direction.

A couple of scoops of raspberry swirl in a waffle cone and a cool patch of grass in the shade helped me chill. But I was the first one to snap my helmet back on. If I hadn't been Vince's tandem partner, I might have gone on ahead of my siblings. I set a fast pace for home. I took us up the connector to the highway. We flew down the ramp toward home.

"Whee-hee! We're on the high-a-w-a-a-y!" The twins cheered from their seats in the carrier, hands up in the wind.

Vince and I began to pull away from Robert and Lil.

"Hey, hey. Not so fast with the precious cargo!" Lil called.

"Can't go fast! Too much twin in the trunk!" I called. "But we'll beat you home, for sure."

"Not by much!" Lil insisted. It was funny to look back and see her neck and neck with Robert.

"Vince, you ready?" I asked.

"Oh yeah."

We biked out. Best we could with the extra weight.

I do a lot of things with my brother. Home stuff. School stuff. Bike-shop stuff. But there is no place on earth that we are better together than on the tandem. We had perfectly smooth road and wide-open space to travel. I had to laugh when I remembered Lil saying, "Dad always says the highway is fastest." It was.

"We should come out more often!" I shouted.

"You say when!" Vince called back.

It was true. He'd go anytime.

"Soon!" I said. "Who knows how long the shortage will last? Ha! Picking it up now," I called. "We are *two* with the machine!"

24

I AM NOT MAGICAL. THAT'D BE RIDICULOUS. BUT sometimes I can sense that something is up. This isn't about my sharp hearing. This happens closer to my bones. By the time we got off the highway I just knew it; something was going to be different at home.

The nanny goats were all up at the gate doing a nervous sort of dance. Everybody-to-the-left, now everybody-to-the-right. Something or somebody was around. Vince knew it too.

"What's going on?" he said. "And where are the dogs?"

"I don't know. Good-ness! Great-ness!" I called.

Out of the corner of my eye, I saw Greatness

lift her head for just a second. Deaf, old Goodness couldn't hear me. They were both bowing outside the Bike Barn door. Noses to the sill, haunches in the air. I clapped my hands. Greatness looked at me and wagged her tail. Goodness looked up and did the same. There was something way more interesting than me over there by the door.

"Hey, Vince, get the twins out of the carrier, will you? I'm going to unlock the shop."

I ran into the house and grabbed the shop key. I came jogging, bound for the shop door. I figured I'd let Goodness and Greatness go inside. Quench their curiosity. But I changed my mind. I veered past the dogs and headed toward the back fence. Maybe the Spive had something to do with all the weirdness. Maybe he'd borrowed Gloria Cloud again.

Oh no! What if he's done something to Lil's mural? Would he?

I hustled. I looked back over my shoulder to see if the dogs had followed me. A voice rang out.

"*Watch it!*"

Too late. I ran my groin straight into the

front wheel of a bicycle.

Make that a copsicle.

"Ugh! Runks!" I crumpled.

"Whoa! Dewey!" Runks took several crazy hops to keep his bike from going over. "Oh, terribly sorry. Ay-yi-yi! That *has* to be excruciating!"

I groaned. "Y-you're tell-in' me-e-e . . ." Trails of pains shot up my core. I bent forward and leaned on the side of the barn. "Ugh . . . oh. Ugh."

"I'm glad I wasn't going any faster," Runks said. "Though I suppose it isn't much consolation to you." The dogs came. Wagging. Licking. Woofing. Runks patted them while I attempted to breathe normally. Vince and the twins arrived at the scene of my misery. Robert and Lil came right behind them.

"Runks? What's going on?" Lil asked. (I hoped he would not make some town-crier announcement about the details of our crash.) "Dewey, are you all right? You look like you're about to get sick."

"Oh-h . . ." Robert spoke in a low growl. "I recognize that posture."

"Yes, I am afraid we had a . . . *compromising* collision," Runks said. "Man versus wheel."

"Groin versus wheel," said Vince.

"Oh," said Lil. "What a drag, hey, Dew?"

Runks scratched his head. "Neither of us was looking. Amazing. It was so precise," he said. "We probably couldn't duplicate that if we tried."

"Oh-h." I drew a difficult breath. "Let's. Not. Ever. Try."

Runks set a hand on my shoulder. "All you can do is wait it out."

I gave him a nod and weathered another wave of shooters.

Lil got right back to business. "Runks, why are you here? Did something happen?"

"I'm *not* here in response to a call, if that's what you mean," Runks offered. "I was just hoping to find someone in the shop."

"Oh. Is Officer Macey with you?" She looked beyond him. "We saw him just a while ago. He said he was coming on duty."

"Officer Macey has been assigned a split shift today," Runks said. "He comes on in an another hour or so. The Rocky Shores PD has made some changes. Perhaps you've seen the papers?" He sounded gloomy. "We've had a few robberies recently."

"No!" said Robert.

"Like when our bikes got stole?" Eva asked.

"Very much like that," Runks told her. "Some . . . uh . . . *items* are missing from the police impound lot over on Dogtown Road," he said. "That's the holding space for larger unclaimed items."

"Larger unclaimed items?" Vince cocked his head.

"Sure. Things like abandoned cars, runaway canoes, rowboats . . ."

"Bikes," I croaked.

"Bingo!" said Runks. "We had twelve in our possession at one point. They've gone missing now, a few at a time."

"Oh my gosh . . ." Lil muttered.

"Bikes," I said again. I straightened up as much as I could. I turned and hobbled back to the Bike Barn door and shoved the key into the lock. The dogs were back to sniffing at the sill.

Vince streamed past me, saying, "I'll check the paddock." I heard the fence creak as he vaulted over it.

I jiggled the key, turned it hard, and the lock popped open. Robert and I rolled the door aside together. In went the dogs, sniffing and wagging. They scratched at the sill and seemed to find something edible along the bearing track. Inside the shop, I let my eyes adjust. Nothing seemed off to me. Vince pounded the paddock door from his side and I opened it.

"Anything?" I asked.

"If something is gone, I don't know what it is."

"Same here," I said. Robert shrugged in agreement. The lineup of bikes on the south wall looked undisturbed.

"Did you think something would be amiss?" Runks asked.

"Well," I said. "Coming home, I just had this feeling. . . ." I already sounded lame, so I went on. "We were gone for a while. We don't usually do that. Then we got back and the animals were being weird. And just now, when you said there have been bike thefts, it's just—"

"Well, you have a lot of bikes to worry about!"

"Yes. We do," I said, and I caught Lil in a little eye roll.

"Anyway, it appears that all is well," Runks said. "When I saw the shop was closed, I took a quick lap around the place just to see if anyone was here, thus my coming around the barn like I did. Sorry again, Dewey. I hope that pain has subsided." I gave him a thumbs-up. Runks went on. "But it's funny, I was sure I heard someone *somewhere* nearby."

"Maybe just *the neighbor. . . .*" Lil jabbed a thumb toward Mr. Spivey's yard. "And you know we're used to him, so don't worry."

"Oh, by the way, Lilly Marriss." Runks turned to face her. "Looks like something incredible is going up on that wall back there."

"In progress," she said. "Or maybe in *process*. But thank you."

I caught a wave of guilt. I should really go out and see what she was up to. The compressor seemed to be resting lately. But she still had possession.

Runks went on, "Please invite me to the unveiling."

"If there is an unveiling, Runks, you'll be on the list, I promise," said Lil. "So can we all agree that all the beasts around here got stirred up over nothing?" She turned to look all around the shop. It seemed she was right. Even the dogs had backed off from the sill. They stood looking up the stairs now.

"Hey, mutts, we all know you're not going up there." I laughed at them. They wagged and kept licking their chops. My guess was that they'd found one of those wonderful things in the doorsill that dogs just love to eat. Ants. Mouse turds.

"So, Runks, you wanted something from the shop?" I said.

"Quite right." He changed character and spoke out one side of his mouth. "I'm traveling without a spare," he admitted. He shook his head in mock shame.

"Shouldn't *ever* happen," I said in my deepest, most serious tone.

"Mea culpa, mea culpa!" Runks said. "And

Officer Macey would shame me for it too, if he knew. Preparedness seems to be a motto of his. Thing is, I swear I had a tube in my kit yesterday." He paused. "Strangest thing. Be that as it may, I wondered if you'd sell me one. Or two?"

I turned to the bench. I pulled two inner-tube boxes off the shelf. "Here you go," I said.

"Grand!" Runks said. "Now, I can either pay you cash out of my own pocket or go through proper procedures with a purchase order from the PD and bring you a check tomorrow."

"Tomorrow is fine," I said. I was being Dad again, in a distracted sort of way. Something was still bothering me. I stood there in the shop, puzzling. Looking back at the shelf with all the inner-tube boxes on it. I barely managed to say good-bye to Runks before Lil and the twins walked him out.

"Everything cool, Boss Man?" Robert stood just behind me.

"Yep. Yep. Everything is cool," I said.

The Boss Man is in control.

Vince and I stayed in the shop after Robert left. We both wanted to finish up the jobs we had started. Then, of course, I got sidetracked tending to several pickups. Eventually, I found myself staring at the shelf again. This time, I had the inventory list in front of me.

This does not match up.

"Hey, Vince," I said. "I'm pretty much doing all the blowouts that come in, right?"

"What's your question?" He sounded annoyed.

"Have you been using any inner tubes?"

"Nope." He started to shake his head. "You can't blame me for—"

"No, wait, Vince. That's not what I meant. In fact, I-I'm sorry for that stuff," I said. My brother was looking right at me now. I came so close to telling him what I was thinking. Then I just couldn't. I held up the inventory list and twisted the truth like a pretzel. "Th-this kind of explains it. Now that I'm keeping track," I said. "We're all set."

"Okay," Vince said. He wore a sort of strange look on his face. Then again, I knew I was being weird, lying and all.

"Hey, listen, I was thinking about what Runks

told us. About that theft at the impound?"

"Yeah."

"Let's just double-check ourselves when we lock up. And let's move all the bikes from the paddock in."

Vince gave me a sickish look. It was a big job.

"I know, I know. We'll cram 'em in here," I said. "There's room for a few more under the stairs. It's just for peace of mind—"

"Yeah, yeah," said Vince. "I'll drag them to the door. You find the space."

25

I LAY ON MY BACK IN THE ATTIC ROOM. VINCE twitched in his sleep in his bed just a few feet away. I felt guilty for not telling him what I knew. If he told Lil—even accidentally—she'd think I'd somehow lost control of things in the Bike Barn. And I hadn't. But we were being robbed—just a little. I was sure of it.

It sounded crazy—*robbed just a little*. "And who does that?" I whispered in the dark. "Who steals from us just a little bit at a time?"

The Spive. Not much of a mystery.

And what's a few bike parts between neighbors?

I tried it on, but it didn't have the same ring as when Dad said it.

What did the Spive want with bike parts, anyway? As far as I knew he didn't own a bike. Maybe he's started hoarding, I thought. Maybe he sees bikes becoming valuable. Maybe he's reselling. Maybe there's an evil, bike-dealing Spive-cousin across town. . . .

And just when was he getting this done? Sure, there were times he'd spooked us by walking into the shop, like the day he wanted the mower. But wouldn't we have seen him take something? Suddenly I thought of the money in the tin.

"Stupid!" I said, and I hopped up in the night. I hustled on tiptoe down the stairs and grabbed the shop key from the hutch.

"Goodness! Greatness!" I hissed to them. "Come on, dogs! Wanna go out? Once more before bedtime. I know you've got it in you!"

Not four feet outside our door, Greatie's ears stood up. She rumbled, then wagged. She barked. "What's up, girl?" I asked. I looked at Goodness. He was sniffing the air. Suddenly both dogs bolted. They ran to the barn and crouched at the sill.

"Not this again," I moaned. Then the dogs turned and ran around the side of the barn. "Dogs! Hey, hey!" I called and whistled. I trotted after them but just for a few paces. It was dark, and I didn't want to run into anything that might be—oh, say—the height of my lap again. I heard a few clanks and bumps at the back of the barn, then some rustling that seemed to whisper, *bend and scurry, bend and scurry.*

The Spive.

I strained, tried to make out his form along the fence or in his dooryard. Oh, it would have been fun to hit him in the eyes with a flashlight and crank out a nice, innocent-sounding, "Whatcha doin', Mr. Spivey?" Of course, I didn't *have* a light, and besides, everything was still. It's not like I'd catch him with much booty tonight, I thought. The Bike Barn was locked up tight and I knew it. I stood there for a moment waiting for *something*. I just expected one more sound to come through the dark somehow. All was quiet.

Meanwhile, the dogs had taken off down the hill toward the pasture. Disappeared into the darkness. There was always something to chase. I gave another whistle in their direction. Of course, Goodness couldn't hear, and Greatie was not perfectly obedient. I went to unlock the shop.

Inside the Bike Barn I pulled the light switch. I grabbed the peppermint tin and took a quick look inside at the loose roll of bills—start-up cash for the next day. The fluorescent hadn't even come completely on when I turned it off again. As I headed out I heard something behind me. Made me jump in my skin. I flicked the light back on. One of my tidy stacks of twenty-four-inch inner tubes had fallen over onto the workbench. I stood still, wondering.

Did I do that? I wasn't even over there. Naw, I don't think I did that.

A split second later, I heard dog breath at the door. Goodie and Greatie, back from the chase. They ran right inside, put their noses in the air and stopped at the stairs to the loft. They stood wagging their tails and taking small leaps off their front paws.

I knew they wouldn't go up, but I decided to

give it a look. I popped my head up into the dim light of the loft. My eye went straight to the moon-bright square of sky at the hay door.

Open.

I crossed the loft and looked out. Three feet below me was the flat surface of the scaffold. I smelled fresh paint.

Oh, Lilly Marriss. You built our thief a stairway.

26

I RECYCLED THE LINE I'D USED ON VINCE WHEN I spoke to Lil the next morning.

"Hey," I said. I met her in the upstairs hall outside the bathroom. "I've been thinking about what Runks said. About that bike theft?"

"At the impound lot?" she said. "I've been thinking about that too."

"W-well, we've got a similar situation," I said. "A lot of bikes in one place." I sounded like the *embodiment of responsibility*.

"Yeah . . . I noticed you moved everything in last night," she said.

Keeping tabs on me . . .

"I thought it was smart," she added.

"I'm double-checking the entrances," I said. I

was careful not to be a jerk about the next part. "I forgot all about the hay door last night."

Lil's eyes popped wide open. "Oh, and with the scaffold up—my heck!" she said, and she bit her lip.

"Lil, I think we have to drag it back a few feet every night. Just in case. And I'll help you, and I'll move it back in the mornings," I said.

She seemed to stop and think about it. "I can do it," she said. "I moved it by myself in the first place. I'll do it. Dew, this isn't about something in particular, is it?"

"Oh, no," I lied. "Crime prevention. That's all."

"Hey, by the way, I'm almost ready to spray again. I'm going to need to hand off Angus and Eva. Probably tomorrow."

"That's cool," I said. I swung around the banister and headed down the stairs. Robert was tapping on the kitchen door and I let him in.

"Back so soon?" I said. "What did you do? Camp out in the pasture with Sprocket?"

"Do I stink that bad?" He sniffed his clothes

then said, "As a matter of fact, I spent the night at the bakery." He held up a wax bag. "Well, that's actually a lie. But I did go early just for these. Fresh bagels."

I let out an appreciative groan. I don't know about other families, but bread was something of a treat for us during the crunch. We could cook. But we didn't have a baker in the house. Lil had gone for grains and crackers at Shoreland's because they kept better.

"Do you think these bagels will get me into trouble with the big sis?" Robert whispered.

I said, "It's worth the risk."

Robert and I began toasting bagels. The smell was good enough to wake the dead—or at least to get several of my siblings down the stairs. Lil came with Angus and Eva right behind her, calling, "What's that smell?"

I ran out and rang the bell for Vince just in case he was daydreaming out at the goat shed. "*Nobody* should miss these," I said, and I sliced open another cinnamon-raisin for the toaster.

When she realized Robert was responsible for

the great smell in the house, Lil looked a little like a horse about to refuse a jump. She did not take a bagel.

"By the way, did you tell him?" she asked me. She grabbed a brush and pulled Eva's hair together behind her head.

"Tell who what?"

"Tell Robert. About working in the Bike Barn?"

"Oh. Oh, yeah!" And there I was tucking food into my cheek again so I could get the words out quickly. (Mom would kill me, I thought.) "Robert, I meant to tell you yesterday. But everything was so crazy, I forgot."

"Dewey! You forgot? That was two days ago!" Lil took over. "Robert," she said, "the Bike Barn is going to pay you. *Retroactively.*"

"Oh, no." Robert looked at me then at Lil then back at me again. "I'm a novice! I approached you, Dewey. Oh, you can't—"

"No. Not up for discussion," Lil said.

"Will you discuss eating this bagel? It has your name on it," Robert replied. He handed Lil her breakfast and she took it.

"I just can't believe you're here on a Sunday," Lil told him.

"That's funny coming from the family that takes no time off," Robert said, and that was the moment that Vince came in the door with his milk buckets.

"Our work is our play," said Vince, with a raging lack of enthusiasm. He walked by me, no hands free, and stole a bite of the bagel I was holding. He chewed and swallowed. "You've got people," he said to me, meaning there were customers at the Bike Barn door. "I'll meet you two suckers out there as soon as I get this cooked and cooled," he said.

Robert was a good mechanic. He was learning fast. He followed Dad's cheat sheets. He could even duplicate harder jobs after seeing them done once through. He also had strong hands when it came to a tire wrench. It was right that we were paying him. We had a third mechanic in the shop again, and Vince and I were both happy about it.

Midmorning, Officer Macey surprised us at

the open door. He carried a wheel hooked on his index finger.

Robert greeted him.

"Ha!" Macey laughed. "They've put you to work, huh?"

Robert nodded. "Here to learn," he said. "Maybe I'll master the Eight Rules for Fixing Anything and change my career path. I think the Marrisses are on to something with this bike biz."

Macey turned to me. "I came to ask a favor," he said. "Any chance I could snag the next twenty minutes or so with your truing stand?" He showed me the wheel. "I hit a rock and put a bulge in the rim. I pinched it back but I think the wheel went out in the process," he said. He glanced at the stand. I had a bike up. "Oh. But you're in the middle of something, aren't you?"

"Yeah, but that's okay. I'll pull it down and just change the order I do things today. No big deal."

So the shop was crowded. It felt great. Even Vince seemed happier. I turned to the spindles. Bikes were still coming in at a steady rate and we had a broad sampling of jobs to get to. But I was hung up on one.

Gilmartin.

I just wanted that bike gone. Vince was busy. But I could install a derailleur. I decided to knock off Gilmartin, so to speak. I reached for the small cardboard box at the back of the bench. It didn't feel right. I flipped the lid off and stopped cold.

Four. Empty. Corners.

"No! No! No!" I said. "Can't be! Can't be! How in the—" I swore several times in a row. I pushed at the box, lifted up the spindles to look under the papers.

"What? What happened?" Macey looked up from the truing stand. Robert froze, holding several bearing rings in his hands. Vince came inside.

"I-I had a part set aside for—" I caught myself. I stopped to think.

Okay, this is a cop. A cop who doesn't care for your thieving neighbor. If you say it's been stolen, everything's going to change here . . . and what about Dad and the whole neighborly stance thing?

The thought of the lie was turning my face red.

I could feel it. I did it anyway.

"Uh . . . I set something aside and now . . . I can't find it," I said. At least that was true.

"What is it?" Robert asked. "I'll help you look." He dropped the rings into the grease bath and wiped his hands on a rag.

"It's a derailleur. A *nice* one. I promised the customer an upgrade."

"Tough customer," Vince said. "Scary customer . . ." His nostrils flared.

"I remember you saying so," Robert said.

"I hate to even ask, but *how* nice a derailleur?" Macey said.

"Very. Forged aluminum upper body on a carbon-fiber outer plate."

"Oh. Ouch." Macey winced.

"It has to be here. We'll just have to find it," Robert said.

So we searched. What a charade. I was miserable. But I felt stuck. And it was killing me to think that in this case, the Spive possibly had no idea of the value of his most recent grab. This was not the same as being robbed just a little.

I was embarrassed to do it, but I called Bocci Bike to see if they had another one. They didn't. I was afraid now. Afraid I'd never get rid of Gilmartin. I'd have to face his wrath again. . . .

"Look, I might be able to help you," Macey said. "I'm biking up to Centertown today. My old stomping grounds." He grinned. "There's a bike shop up there."

"Yeah, I've heard of Centertown Cycle."

"That's the place. A guy I went to high school with started it up. So I'll stop in and ask what he has for high-end derailleurs."

"But Centertown is a haul."

"Twenty-five miles or so." Macey shrugged. "I bike everywhere. For me, that trip's nothing. Besides, you just did me a favor with this baby." Macey lifted his newly trued wheel off the stand. "Write down the name, model number, whatever you've got. A second choice if you've got one. You might as well make a list of anything else you need too. I can't promise anything. But it's worth a try."

Too nice!

I offered him the money up front. I thought

Dad would do the same. But Macey said, "I'll let my guy know you're good for it. I'll stop by tomorrow before my shift. Hopefully I'll have something for you."

"Thanks, Officer Macey. Thanks more than you know," I said.

27

IT TOOK ME FOREVER TO FALL ASLEEP THAT night. Bedtime is a bad hour to let anything ugly creep into your thoughts. I was thinking about Mr. Gilmartin. What if Officer Macey couldn't get me that part? For sure, Gilmartin would chew me up and spit me out in little pieces all over my own yard. He'd bad-mouth the Bike Barn, and the Marrisses would be mud. . . .

Then it hit me. Wasn't this solvable? With or without help from Officer Macey and Centertown Cycle? Wasn't that derailleur for Gilmartin's bike just sitting in a box or a drawer at the house next door?

I ran a quick daydream there in the night. I pictured going right up to the Spive's back door and knocking.

"*Look, you can fling that arm and peck that finger at me, but I know that you have something that belongs to me. If you just hand it over now, I'll forgive it along with the dozens of eggs and pints of berries you've taken from my family. I'll forgive your crabbing and demanding and your stinkin' slamming door. . . .*"

The door. That was it! That was the sound I had waited to hear the night the dogs had run off. Right after *bend and scurry*, the Spive's screen door *always* banged shut.

A new creepy feeling washed over me. What if the Spive was not the thief? The thought made my guts flip. But who? And why wouldn't they go ahead and wipe us out instead of just pinching this and that? I began to wonder about all the people coming and going, the Bike Barn customers, even our milk-and-egg customers. Had I missed a serial shoplifter? Had I gone to the house for lunch and stayed too long without locking up? Thoughts swam. It seemed like it had to be someone who was around a lot.

Then I had the sickest thought of all.

What about Robert? He's around. He knows the shop. He knows our dogs—

"No, no, no," I whispered into the dark, and waved my hands in the air to erase the thought. It was stupid anyway.

A little bit at a time.

It *had* to be Mr. Spivey. That was his MO, and surely he was clever enough to stop a screen door from slamming in the night.

28

IN THE MORNING, THE YARD WAS BUSY. THE smell of fried eggs wafted across the lawn from Mr. Spivey's open kitchen window. Shameless.

"How about a slab of fried inner tube with them eggs?" I mumbled.

It was barely eight o'clock and there were three customers standing at the Bike Barn door. I watched at the open window as Angus and Eva stopped to say hello to them on their way from the coop. Had to laugh. Each twin carried a basket of eggs. Each twin was wearing nothing but underpants. All three customers chatted with them and admired the eggs while the Athletes strutted nearby, as if to say, "Look what *we* made!" At least we offered entertainment while people waited.

Then who should come Rollerblading onto the scene but Gilmartin.

Oh, joy.

I reached and pulled the key from the corner cupboard, and I walked out the door.

The four customers stood in an orderly way. One behind the other. "Good morning," I said, sort of covering them all. I nodded at my personal favorite at the end of the line and said, *"Mr. Gilmartin."*

He took that as a signal to speak. "I didn't get a call. I was checking to see if—"

"These folks are ahead of you," I said. "But just so you know, your bike isn't done yet."

"I figured you'd call if it was, but I was taking the highway today and, well, here you are at the exit. Just thought I'd stop and see."

I almost said that I hoped it'd be done later that day. But the truth was, I had no idea if I could even get the part. And what would I do if I couldn't? Gilmartin would surely have a piece of me—

"Excuse me, are you going to unlock the

shop?" I looked into the face of a woman I recognized from the desk at the town library. She shoved her bike forward just slightly and stuck her chin out toward the Bike Barn door. Her bicycle chain dragged in the dust.

"Y-yes," I said. But before I did anything, I leaned around the first three customers and said, "Mr. Gilmartin, *we'll call you.*"

He left and I checked the three new jobs in. I told them about the backlog. No one was happy, but they all seemed to get it.

I guess Officer Macey must have rolled up around eight thirty. He rode his copsicle right inside the open door, then stuck on his brakes. He stood balancing on his pedals for a few seconds before he jumped down to the floor with a thud. "Good news!" he said. Then he made a *yikes* sort of face and added, "And bad news, too."

"Let's have it," I said. I was sure he had everything but the derailleur.

"Here's the good news." He held a plain box with a rubber band around it up and gave it a gentle shake. "The derailleur. *Exact* model."

Vince, behind me at the paddock door, said, "Hallelujah!"

"Yes!" I said. "I can't believe it."

"Yeah, well, I can't believe the *price*." He gave me the bad news—half again what I'd paid for the one that'd disappeared.

"Ugh," I said.

"You don't have to keep it," Macey insisted. "Your choice. Centertown Cycle said they're just as happy to have it in their inventory."

"No. I have to do it."

"You already gave Gilmartin a price," Vince said.

"Yep. I'll eat this. I'm so glad to have it."

We figured out my tab. Horrible, but at least we had money. I jogged back to the house for it. Robert had arrived by the time I returned. I felt a little wave of shame when I saw him. I felt bad for the split second I'd suspected him, but I let it go.

"That's a lot of lettuce," he said. He watched me hand Macey the stack of bills.

"Officer Macey got that part I needed," I said.

"Made my day, and it's still early!"

"Oh, that's great," Robert said. "Expensive little gizmo, huh?"

"Very," I said.

"It's hard to believe that it isn't here *some-where*," Robert puzzled. He'd never quite given up the hunt, I could tell.

"It could turn up," I said, not believing my words for a second. "But I'm not thinking about it anymore," I said. "I'm going to install the new one and I'm going to call the guy *today*. He'll have no more reason to harass me or insult us."

"You know, Dewey, there are different kinds of crimes," said Macey.

"Y-yeah?" I felt glued in place. Where was he going with this? Had he found me out?

"If someone disturbs your peace, or challenges you unfairly in the shop, there is no reason you can't call it in. It'll take us a while to get here, these days. But we'll help you handle it," he said.

"Th-thanks," I said. "Really. I appreciate that."

Macey looked at Robert. "You hanging around

here again all day?" he asked.

Robert grinned. "Another day with the geniuses! I love my new job. I'm sponging up the mechanical know-how."

Macey stretched his arms up. Let out a throaty groan. "Well, just another day of ordinary mayhem for me."

"Yeah, how's it going?" I asked. "Officer Runkle told us a bike thief hit the impound lot."

Macey smacked the workbench with the heel of his hand. "Makes us look like such chumps!" His face turned red under his white-blond hair. "So help me, I'm going to be the one who breaks that case."

"I took it as a warning," I said. "I'm pulling all the bikes here inside." That'd be a hard thing to explain to a customer, I thought. "So many repairs. Speaking of which . . ."

"Yeah, we'd better get to it, hey, Boss Man?" Robert said.

"Better," I agreed.

Macey squared up the stack of bills for Centertown Cycle in his hands. I thought about the long trip he'd taken up there.

"Thanks," I told him. "Thanks for everything."

Later, it felt good to watch Mr. Gilmartin ride off "into the sunset, never to be seen again," I whispered to Robert. I swept my hands after my favorite customer, who was well out of the driveway now. "Good riddance!" I added.

Robert laughed and then said, "You're really good at this. You're good with the business of the bikes. That can be even harder than repairing them."

"Well, thanks," I said. It was a good moment for the temporary manager of the Marriss Bike Barn.

29

"OKAY, THAT'S IT!" ANGUS TOLD US. HE AND EVA came jumping down the loft stairs into the bike shop. "Lil said that's the last time we can go up and in. She's ready to spray it now."

"And we can't get sprayed," Eva added.

Timing is everything. We heard the compressor fire up.

"Thar she blows!" Robert said, and he laughed out loud.

"Yep, you need to stay out of her way," I told the twins. I raised my voice and growled at them. "That means *you're* with *me*! RO-AR-r-r-r!"

"Wait, wait! Dewey, Lil said to ask you if you can make the hay door stay shut while she's spraying it," Eva said. "Because the hooking thing broke and we can't shut it."

"The latch?"

Eva looked at me. "It's just off." She shrugged. "I think it's lost now."

I went up to have a look for myself. Some of the hardware had been knocked clean away. I had to wonder when it'd happened. It would have to be replaced, and I knew I could find a new latch set in the kitchen drawer. Dad kept that sort of stuff around, what with our many fences, gates, and doors. I didn't want to make a trip to the house just then. So I did a makeshift thing with some bailing twine through the old eye screws and just tied it shut.

"Is it okay?" Eva asked.

"It's *o-kay*!" I growled, and I carried her down the stairs like a sack of potatoes.

For the next hour or so Eva sat on the workbench getting into everything and asking a hundred questions, especially if this or that part could go on the new bike I would someday build her. Angus sort of ran in and out of the paddock for no particular reason. Eventually Eva began to sing "The Song That Gets on Everybody's Nerves." Then Angus nearly took out Robert as he was wheeling a job up to the front, which Robert was nice about, of course. But when Eva knocked over the grease bath with her foot, that's when I said, "*Okay!* We're going outside!"

Eva gave me a pout as I mopped up the mess with a rag.

"Let's go see what Lil's doing," I said, trying to keep it cheery. "Vince! Robert. Come on. Everybody, let's take a breather."

Lil was pretty focused. She was up on the scaffold, mask over her face, bandanna on her head. She used the sprayer and swept greasy blue paint over her paper flying figures. She'd made her way almost all the way across the very top section. Still a lot of spraying to go, I thought.

"What a project," Robert said near my ear.

"I think the sun will set before she's done," I said.

"That one is me," Angus shouted over the hum of the compressor. He pointed to one of the shapes. "And underneath there is lots of painting. And when the blue paint dries, Lil's going to peel away the paper."

"Oh, I get it," said Robert.

Lil stopped. Time to move the scaffold a foot or two. She pulled down her mask and grinned. She shut off the compressor and swung down to the ground. "I didn't even know you guys were here," she said. "Everything okay?"

"Yep," I said. I stepped up, and she let me help her move the scaffold.

"Good. Dewey, Vince, can you guys cook some pasta for dinner, but don't wait for me, okay? I'm kind of rushing to finish spraying. This needs a day to dry and they say rain is coming. Maybe tomorrow night."

"Rain! Who remembers rain?" said Vince. It had been a long time.

We didn't have much choice but to wrap things up early in the Bike Barn, what with Angus and Eva in our full care. They were underfoot as I sent a few more bikes home. I skipped sorting the orders for the next day.

"Hey, Robert, pretty safe night to hang for supper," I said.

"You mean because your sister doesn't like me and she won't be around anyway?" He laughed.

"She doesn't *not* like you," I said. "Lil's just—"

"She has a lot on her shoulders," Robert said.

"Yeah."

"And she doesn't like you," Vince said with a twisted grin.

We went in to the garden laughing. The twins had spent more time there recently than Vince and I had. They knew where to find the ripe stuff, even under a wicked growth of weeds. Vince took a handful of wild carrots and said, "I'm going out to challenge the goat." That meant that he was going to try to distract Sprocket long enough with the carrots that he might get the old goat's shelter mucked.

"Don't get butted," Angus warned.

We went ahead with dinner without Lil, like she'd said. Afterward, Robert helped the twins with the dishes and I searched through the kitchen drawer and found a latch set for the hay door. I'd get to it later. Lil didn't realize it, but right now she was serving guard up there on her scaffold. No way was the Spive going to slither up to the hay door with Lilly Marriss standing in his path. With a paint gun, I thought, and it made me laugh—just to myself. I swept the floor and took the recycling down to the basement. Vince and Robert turned on the TV to catch the news.

"Man, all this footage of highway traffic," Robert mumbled. "It makes me think it's happening *now* and they are about to tell us the shortage is over."

"Yeah," said Vince. "Those are old-time movies."

I took the call from Mom and Dad that night. I was glad to hear from them, but in truth, their calls had become kind of same-old, same-old. They were still stuck and we were still here. We'd stopped talking about the thing we all wanted, the thing that wouldn't come: fuel.

I talked shop with Dad and told him about having Robert work for us. That was news, but of course I couldn't tell him the story of Gilmartin's derailleur disappearing, and how Macey had rescued me on that one. I wanted to keep Dad and everyone believing that I was handling the Bike Barn just fine. It wasn't my fault that we lived next door to a thief.

Mom and Dad were sorry not to speak to Lil, but they were happy that she was out there pushing along on the art thing. "She needs that," Mom said. "It'll be exciting to come home and see what she's done. But it's also crazy to think that we've missed so much."

I gave the phone to the twins. I noticed that even they had less to say. I think it must have been Mom's idea to sing with them, and I heard, "Flap your wings to the left, flap your wings to the right, but wait little bird, you're not ready for flight . . ."

It was after dark when Lil practically tumbled in the door. "I finished!" she said. She slumped into a chair at the table.

"How could you see?" I asked.

"*Pfft!* Well, I adjusted. But I almost didn't have to see! I was basically spraying the entire side of the barn. So, as long as I could find that . . . the details are all underneath the paper."

"Did you do the peel-the-paper part?" Eva asked.

"No! And it's killing me! I can't wait!" She grinned and clapped her palms against Eva's. "But not until tomorrow or the next day, when the blue paint is dry," Lil said. Then she noticed Robert, who'd fallen asleep on the living-room floor. Eva had covered him with a beach towel. "Oh, what is he? The largest sleepover friend this house has ever seen?" Lil said.

"Well, I don't think he planned to stay . . . but, yeah, it turns out he sleeps through quite a lot," I said.

"Everything," said Vince, who had been doing some snoozing himself.

"Yeah," said Eva. "Goodness even stepped on him."

"And Greatie gave him a bath," Angus added.

Lil looked at me and made a silent laugh. "Maybe he's *faking*," she piped. She waited, then said, "Nope. Guess we have a corpse!" She was in a great mood after her big art day.

"I'm sure I can wake him," I said. "But do we care?"

Lil shrugged. "Fine. He stays. But just tonight, Dewey. Then it's up to Mom and Dad to decide if they'll let you keep him."

Vince howled at that. He covered his mouth. We all looked down at Robert Deal. He hadn't moved a hair.

I set Lil's rewarmed dinner on the table and she reached for it with an appreciative moan. I jerked back the plate and said, "You're filthy! Do I have to be the parents? Go wash your hands!" Lil laughed out loud.

Later, as I was following Lil and Vince up the stairs to bed, I remembered the hay door. Ugh. I thought about waiting for morning, but it was an easy job and I didn't want to risk leaving it. I turned and headed back down.

"Where you going, Dew?" Lil whispered.

"I forgot to put the new latch set on the hay door. I just tied it shut earlier. I'll sleep better if I know it's secure."

"I'll come and help you," Lil said.

"Naw, I'll take Vince," I said. He was easier to work with.

"Not me!" Vince complained. He stood at the top of the stairs saying, "I'm asleep. I'm asleep."

"You're standing right there," I said.

"No. I'm just an apparition."

"Vince, come on," I said. "I need you to hold the light. Two minutes—max."

"O-kay-o-kay-o-kay . . ."

Greatness bolted well ahead of us the second she hit the grass. Goodness bunny-galloped after her on his old wobbly legs. We watched them go straight to the barn door. They put their noses to the sill. Again.

"What *is* it with them?" I wondered out loud.

"They're very focused," said Vince. He yawned noisily. "Oh, boy. This bike genius is tired," he said.

"Bike genius," I scoffed.

"Hey, Robert said it. He's right. Seriously. Name a bike repair that I haven't done now. Not mastered, maybe. But what job is there that I can't get through? You too, Dew. What can't you get through? That's my essay."

"What?" I wasn't used to Vince doing this much talking.

"'What the Crunch Did for Me.'"

"Did for you?"

"Yep. Because of the crunch, I can now do a bunch of repairs I couldn't do before. And don't go stealing my idea."

"Your idea?"

"For the essay. When we get back to school, it's mine."

"It's everybody's," I mumbled.

At the Bike Barn door I swept the flashlight across the sill. "Goodie! Greatie! What's the big dog deal here?"

I released the lock and slid the door open. The dogs dove on the track. They snarfed and munched. Vince bent down and took a chunk of something right out of Greatie's mouth.

"Give me some light," he said. I put the beam on the little pinkish red crumb. "Looks like one of those colored dog biscuits," he said.

"Are you sure?" I said. "Better taste it, Vince."

"Not me. I already brushed my teeth." He looked at it one more time. "Weird. It's not the kind we usually get," he said.

A bell went off inside my thick head.

Oh man! The Spive has been bribing the dogs!

I almost said it out loud.

Keeping them busy at the door while he makes his way in and out up above.

We went into the shop. The dogs went right to the bottom of the stairs and stood wagging their tails.

Or is that the way the biscuits come in? Whichever. Time to fix it.

I pulled the chain to turn on the light over the workbench. I had Dad's drill in the charger. It was the last piece of equipment I needed. Then I heard a noise overhead. I looked up at the Trap. It was open. Flecks of hay dust fell through the light and drifted down. I turned up my palm. Watched them land in my hand. The dogs pranced at the bottom of the stairs. They wagged and woofed. I looked at Vince. I put a finger on my lips then slowly pointed upward. He tilted his head and we both waited. I caught more dust in my hand. Vince saw it too. Silently, I mouthed: *The Spive?*

Vince opened his eyes wide. Then his jaw dropped.

"Okay!" I said loudly. Vince jumped. "We're set here. Let's call it a night." I left everything on the bench and encouraged him along with a lot of eyeball language.

"R-right," Vince said. "Let's head in."

"Goodie, Greatie. Come on. Let's go!" I tried not to whistle a happy tune or do anything so dead-giveaway as that. I tried not to rush—had to fight my own racing heart—tried to roll the door closed just like I always did. Once it was shut, Vince whispered, "What are we going to do?"

"Lock up," I whispered back, and I threaded the padlock as calmly as I could and clicked it shut. Then I talked fast. "He's got one way out. I'm going to get there before he does. Quick. Take the dogs to the house. Grab 'em, Vince! Go! Go!" As soon as he had their collars I took off.

I hurried—hopped over the mounds of dry grass

along the side of the barn, all the while thinking, I have no plan, I have no plan. I rounded the corner as fast as I could. Why didn't I bring the light? I was afraid of crashing into Lil's scaffold. Not much moonlight. I dragged my fingers along the building as I went. I found one of the vertical pipes of the scaffold and gripped it. At the same moment something landed with a *thud* on the platform above me. The pipe vibrated in my hand. I crouched down.

What's the plan?

All I could do was startle him. Scare him. I saw his feet catch a rung. The Spive looked huge in the darkness. My heart pounded. I backed up and my arm brushed something—the compressor. I dropped my hand low for balance. My fingers curled around the paint sprayer. I found the trigger.

Oh! Just a reserve. Let there be a reserve. . . .

I held my breath.

The Spive hit the ground then straightened up.

I fired.

The paint flew.

30

I GOT JUST THE ONE SHOT OUT OF THE sprayer.

A yelp of surprise cut the air. There was stumbling and scrambling. I saw a pale head on a bulky form. The crook took off running toward our pasture—*fast*.

Fast, like Mr. Spivey had probably *never* been. Not in his whole life.

"Dewey! What was that?"

I turned quickly. "Who's there? Get the light out of my eyes!" I froze and dropped the paint sprayer where I stood.

"It's us!" Lil swept the light up into her own face. Vince was with her. So was Robert, still blinking away sleep.

"Dew, are you okay? What happened?"

"I sh-shot—"

"Shot what?"

"Shot—p-paint!" I needed to breathe. I took two long draws then spoke again. "H-he was in the loft—"

"Vince said it was Mr. Spivey?" Lil whispered. "This late at night?"

"I *thought* it was Mr. Spivey. Because of all the missing parts—"

"Missing parts?"

I shrank back.

"W-we were losing stuff—just a little at a time—"

"Oh, Dewey! My god!" Lil gasped. She hit me with the light again.

"But listen!" I shielded my face. "It *wasn't* him. He can't run like that. And he can't push the scaffold—" Lil glanced at the scaffold then looked back at me. "And—also—I saw *white*," I said.

"White?"

"White hair." I brushed my head with my hands. "Like *glow-in-the-dark*. You guys, I think it was—"

"*Macey?*" Lil said. "White hair like *Officer Macey*?"

"Macey's your thief?" Robert said. "Oh, holy—"

"'*Your thief*'? Wait! Wait! You *knew* about this?" Lil pushed the question at Robert. I was having the same thought myself. He knew?

"I didn't know anything, not for sure," Robert said. "But I've been around here and I-I saw some things, thought there might be something wrong becau—"

"Oh, Dewey! How could you?" Lil said. "Stuff's been missing? And you hid it from me?" Talk about being the parents. She sounded so disappointed it made the shame rise inside of me.

"I-I thought it was just the Spive." I swallowed. "But *that* couldn't have been." I pointed off into the dark. "That was Macey. I swear it was."

"This is *not* good," Lil said. "None of this is good. We're going back to the house." She began to march. "Angus and Eva are alone, and I want everyone together. In one place. *Now*. Then we sort this out. Get a little *truth*." She stopped suddenly and blocked me with her hand across my chest. "Did you bring in the money? Is that tin still in the barn?"

"I-bro—"

"Is it still in the *barn*, Dewey? It's *not* a trick question!"

"No! It's at the house."

She resumed the march. We followed. My mind raced. I imagined that Macey had stashed his bike somewhere out beyond Sprocket's pasture. I imagined that he was already well up the highway. Piecing it all together only haunted me more. Macey knew bikes. He knew our shop. He could easily put a shoulder into that scaffold and stroll it right up to the hay door. He knew our dogs.

I felt jumpy—a thousand kinds of nervous—and Lil was mad at me on top of it all. I kept looking into the dark behind me.

Robert clapped a hand on my shoulder as we reached the house. "It's okay. It's okay, Boss Man. I got your back," he said.

Lil turned at the door, her face lit up now by the yellow porch light. She gave Robert a stony look. "*I've* got his back," she said.

31

I TWITCHED WITH ADRENALINE—SO MUCH that I'm confused about the exact order of events. I know we locked our doors for the first time in my entire life. Just symbolic, I guess, because we left our windows open to cool the house. I know that Lil called the Rocky Shores PD, and that Officer Runkle arrived quickly by bike. Two more officers followed after him in the one electric wheelie pod the town owned.

I swallowed rocks when I told Runks that I was almost positive that it was Officer Macey. The other two officers looked at each other. I somehow got the feeling that bells were going off for them and for Runks. Lil kept repeating that we did not know anything for certain.

"I sp-sprayed him with blue paint," I said. I drummed my fingers nervously on the top of the table. "It—it would be obvious."

"It's permanent," Lil added. She pushed a few blue stands of hair out of her face and rubbed at a mark on her wrist.

With that, the two cops left. They were in a hurry, as I recall, but I was so jittery everything seemed to move fast. Runks stayed. I spent the next forty minutes or so answering questions about what I thought was missing and how long ago it had begun. All the while Lil paced nearby. She just kept shaking her head at everything I was saying. Robert and Vince sat by and listened. Meanwhile, I heard a few bells of my own.

"It started right around the time the flags went up at the pumps." I thought about it as I spoke. "Right after we found out Mom and Dad wouldn't be back on time. And . . . right after we met Macey. Yeah. That's it, I think. After the night we made clam chowder with Pop and Mattie. At first, I didn't even understand that parts were being taken."

"And that makes sense," Vince blurted. "Because, Runks, I'm a space-shot. Dewey thought it was me losing the parts."

I think that was the only time we laughed. Robert leaned up and patted Vince on the back. I told Runks about the dog biscuits at the door, the scaffold, and the busted latch on the hay door.

"It sounds so stupid now, but I just kept coming back to Mr. Spivey," I said. "Because he just took a little at a time."

When I told Runks about Mr. Gilmartin's derailleur—that I was pretty sure now that Macey had swiped it and then sold it back to me— Runks made a low, disgusted sound in his throat. "Ignoble," he said. I'd never heard that word, but I didn't have to ask what he meant.

"One other thing, then," Runks said. "What about your cash? Was there ever any money missing?"

I took a long breath in, avoided eye contact with Lil, and admitted it. "I'm not sure," I said. "I wasn't that . . ."

"Meticulous?" Robert helped me out.

"Right. B-but if he did take money, it was just like with everything else." I knew I sounded defensive. "It wasn't enough to make me flat-out suspicious. I-I just can't believe I'm sitting here saying all of this." My lips felt numb. "Macey's a cop! I thought he was our *friend*."

I think that's when Runks took a call out on the porch for privacy. Hard not to try to listen. I heard him talking about bikes.

When he came back in, he sat down with me again. He looked pretty stunned, I thought. He rubbed his face with his hands then said, "You were right. You filled Officer Macey's right ear with blue paint."

Across the room, Lil muttered, "Ohmygod, ohmygod, ohmygod . . ."

"They already know?" I said. "It *was* Macey." I wilted forward, my head in my hands. I realized then how much I'd wanted to be wrong.

"The evidence is overwhelming," Runks said. "Marked man, so to speak, thanks to your good aim. It looks like this connects to several investigations." He shook his head. "We have quite a lot of light being shed all at once."

"Oh! Holy!" Robert rocked forward, nearly flew out of his chair. "The bike thefts at the police impound lot!"

My heart pumped. Lil stopped pacing.

Runks might have nodded slightly. "Macey's apartment is full of bicycles, and some other items of interest. He was first on the scene at several robberies—incidences of jimmied doors—and now it appears he may have been the thief."

"But why?" I said. "You said he was the best and the brightest."

"Maybe that's exactly why," Runks said. "Every rookie has a lot to prove, and Macey seemed all out to do just that. But we think he was creating crime scenes, then controlling them to make himself look good."

"Being on the outside and the inside," Robert offered.

"Ew . . . oh, gosh." Lil shivered as if she felt both pain and disgust.

"That derailleur," I mumbled. "Bad guy, good guy."

"I can't say more," Runks said. "But it's possible that the whole story will hit the news as early as tomorrow, anyway. The investigation is sure to go on for months." He waited with a frown on his lips. He looked at Lil, then Vince, then me. Then he sighed. "I hope with all my heart that you understand that he acted alone. I, for one, am proud to work for Rocky Shores. Ours is a *good* department. Above all, please know how sorry I am that I ever brought him to the Marriss Bike Barn."

Lil walked straight over to Runks and hugged him. "How could anybody have known?" she said.

I was counting on her remembering those words.

32

I DIDN'T DO MUCH SLEEPING. I CHECKED ON Angus and Eva at least four times while it was still dark out. No real reason. Coming down from upstairs the final time I saw that Vince had crashed in Dad's armchair. Robert was back on the floor—snoozing. Runks had suggested he stick around. "Another adult in the house," he'd said, and Lil had yielded, even though I knew she was annoyed.

I heard Lil on the phone with Mom and Dad. She stood in the front window, where the dark of night was just beginning to creep away. I was exhausted and amped-up all at the same time. I registered just bits of what she said.

"Bribed the dogs. Got in through the hay door.

Dewey sprayed him. Cops are checking in. Runks will call you as soon as he gets a chance. We're fine. It's supposed to rain, by the way." There was a long pause, then she added, "I'm tired, Mom. I'm just tired. Yep. Love you, too." Lil hung up. She landed on one end of the couch and slumped there. I landed on the other.

"You didn't tell them," I said.

"What?"

"That I knew stuff was missing and didn't say anything."

"Yeah. Well. You look bad, I look bad." She flopped sideways and closed her eyes. She was done talking to me.

I woke to find Vince standing over me and daylight coming in the windows behind him. He stretched his arms above his head and gave the day some heck with a mighty yawn.

"Robert went on home for a shower," he said.

We did the morning milking together, me resting my forehead against Camilla's side. The police were around, wanting a quick look at the crime scene in the light of day. I unlocked the Bike Barn for them, but we stayed out of their way, stealing just a peek around the side of the barn.

I looked at the scaffold. I remembered the body dropping down from it. The scramble on the ground. The flash of white hair. Me, hitting my target . . .

And speaking of my target—or what I *thought* was my target when I'd squeezed that trigger in the dark—there stood Mr. Spivey at the edge of the yard. He had his hands tucked firmly in his pits and he watched the cops through one squinted eye. For just one tiny part of one tiny second, I felt bad for suspecting him. Bike parts—that wasn't his kind of stealing, and now it seemed to me that I should have known better. I turned toward the house with Vince. I felt the handle of the milk bucket in the crease of my fingers. I felt my neighbor's eye on my back.

The twins came in from the coop, and Eva asked, "Why did Officer Runkle and his friends come today?"

"To see the mural," Lil said, without flinching.

"Is this the unbailing?"

"Unveiling," said Lil. "Sure it is. Whatever."

"But you didn't peel off the papers yet."

"They're taking pictures of it already," Angus said. "What about Officer Macey? He didn't come?"

I tried to field that one. "Uh . . . no. He's . . . uh . . ."

"Feeling blue." Vince finished with an amazing snort. It was like all the tension in the room had been drawn right up his nose. It all came out again in a big laughing fit. Lil and I couldn't help but join in. Angus and Eva just smiled because we were laughing.

But I sidled up to Lil and said, "I think we have to tell them."

"You mean *be honest*," she said, and she gave me a hard look.

"Right," I said.

So we gathered up the twins and Lil broke the news. I think our twins felt less betrayed than we did, and luckily, they didn't seem afraid. Maybe that was because they were used to daily egg robberies. But they were full of questions—the kind that are hard to answer.

"Well, but he stole stuff even though he is the police?" Angus said.

"But doesn't he just have the keys to the jail?" Eva asked, her nose wrinkling up. "He could let himself out. Because he *is* the police, right?"

"I'm sure they took the keys away from him," Lil said.

"He brought us lollipops when our bikes got stole," Angus said.

"He was going to find our bikes," Eva added.

He sold me back my own derailleur. I couldn't dump that thought.

Wow. Kindnesses turning to crimes.

"Well, I guess we have two thieves," Eva said. "Mr. Spivey is our thief and now Officer Macey is too."

33

AFTER WE TOLD THE TWINS ABOUT OFFICER Macey, Lil began thrashing through the house chores. She still didn't have much to say to me. I just wanted to get out to the Bike Barn. My oasis. But Runks and the other officers were still wrapping it up out there—inside and outside the barn.

I screwed up the courage to ask Lil about the mural. "Hey, weren't you going to do something out there today? Peel paper?"

She stopped her furious scrubbing of the refrigerator. "My mural is a crime scene," she said. Vince thought that was funny, but he stopped laughing when Lil didn't even break a grin.

"They shouldn't be out there much longer," I said.

"I'm just not that interested in it today." She

226

went ahead with her scouring. I decided to look useful *and* stay out of Lil's way, so I took the compost bucket out and dumped it. When I was rinsing it out at the hose below the kitchen window, I overheard Vince saying, "Come on . . . he didn't tell me either, Lil. And I'm not mad at him. Not at all."

I would have liked to hear her reply. But if she said anything, it was drowned out by a lady who called to me from across the yard.

"Excuse me! Hello! Do you work here?" She pointed at the Bike Barn, and I nodded. She was one of several people waiting with bikes to log in. I set the compost pail on the steps and jogged over to help her. "Service seems a little slow," she said. "Was there some sort of trouble here? I saw the police leaving."

"Everything is okay," I said. We talked about her bike and I pushed it into the shop with the rest.

I'd no sooner started work when Angus and Eva ran the phone out to me. It was Robert. "Boss Man," he said, "hate to tell you, 'cause I know things are probably crazy this morning, but I was feeling cruddy last night and I barely made it home this morning. I've got a stomach bug. I'm off today. Sorry."

I closed my eyes. Felt tired. That all-night adrenaline rush was finally catching up to me. "Sorry for you. Feel better soon, Robert. We'll get by."

Truth was, I needed him. We were pretty backed up. Quitting early one afternoon and not getting started until late the next morning had caused a bike jam. And now we had a fair number of jobs that we simply didn't have parts for. I couldn't even blame that all on Macey. We'd been busy, and we'd run through plenty of parts on our own. And now, I wouldn't have Robert today. I felt a little sandstorm blowing through my oasis.

I sat down in the shop and closed my eyes for just a minute. Should I call Mr. Bocci for parts? Should I run a whole new triage? Do I have to decide?

"Gaw!" I said it out loud. I scrubbed my head with my hands. For the first time all summer— or all crunch—I didn't want to work on bikes. I wanted people to fix their own. You ride it, you repair it! Okay. Bad attitude for a bike mechanic.

Then Vince came through with a bike on his shoulder and headed out to the paddock. "Did you see that sky?" he asked. "It's going to rain." He put the bike on the stand. He twisted one bare toe into the dirt and crouched down to check the crank.

Days can flip on you—sometimes for the better.

If Vince could work, I could work. And I did. I even got into the zone for a while. I was completing jobs and wheeling them to the front. I was on a second wind, and in the middle of it I realized something else. I had one less worry than I'd had the day before. My thief was *caught*! A big chunk of my Bike Barn trouble was over with.

Or at least that's what I thought.

34

I WAS LEANING DOWN TO INSPECT A JOCKEY pulley when my ears picked up on a humming sound. I straightened up and listened. It was coming from the driveway.

Vince hurried in from the paddock. "What is that?" he said.

I stepped outside. The dogs ran by me. I took a look. Then I ducked back in. "Oh. My. Hell." I stared at Vince. "It's a news crew in a wheelie pod."

We could hear two women talking. "O-o-okay, this way. Watch the—uh—ew, I think it's chicken poop, right there. Nice dogs, nice dogs. They seem friendly. Bring it around. Yep, yep. Watch that! Another poop. Oh, and here comes the chicken . . . uh . . . make that two. Cock-a-doodle-doo, fellas!

Okay, okay, let's make sure we get a panoramic of the property . . . and get a clear shot of the door to the shop . . . see if you can get the animals in it. That's a classic. . . ."

"News crew?" Vince said. "W-w-why?"

I thought for a second. "The Officer Macey stuff!" I said. My brother turned into Petrified Vince right before my eyes. "I got this," I said. I grabbed his shoulders and pushed him toward the loft stairs. "Go! Go hide. Disappear!" He was gone in a flash.

"Hello? Hello? We're looking for Dewey Marriss?" A woman in a dressy pink suit came right in the shop door. Microphone in her hand. Goodie wagged his dusty tail into her skirt. *Thwump! Thwump!* Greatie kept going in for a lick at her shin. The camerawoman sidestepped another chicken dropping. The Athletes flapped and scattered.

"Are you Dewey?" The reporter checked her notes. She looked me up and down. "He's about fourteen. Looks like we have our man!"

My memory of the interview is hazy. *Surreal*,

as Lil says. And there was nothing more *surreal* than watching myself on the early evening news. There I was. On the screen. But I could hardly remember it happening. Of course I'd only said two things before Lil had come flying out of the house to shut them down—in no uncertain terms. But they didn't need us. They had their report and their footage. Like Runks had predicted, the story of Officer Macey had hit the news.

The preamble to the report said:

ROCKY SHORES ROOKIE LEFT FEELING BLUE.

Then it really got going:

It was a well-aimed shot that helped put a stop to some mysterious thefts in the quiet town of Rocky Shores last night; specifically, that shot came from a paint sprayer. It happened at this unassuming little bike-repair shop known to locals as the Marriss Bike Barn. Fourteen-year-old Dewey Marriss squeezed the trigger and turned rookie Officer Darren Macey, well, blue.

*   *   *

"Hey! Wasn't that my line?" Vince said.

"Ha! Look at you, Dew!" Angus pointed to the TV.

My face stretched across the screen. A bug flew by my nose. My eyes moved left to right to left again. In our living room, my loyal siblings laughed hysterically. Angus and Eva shouted my name.

The TV station had spliced together footage of me saying the two sentences I'd managed to utter, which were: "W-well, we r-repair bikes." And "W-well, our parts were going missing . . . and stuff . . . and so . . . I wanted to stop that." Again, my two oldest siblings were in spasms.

Okay, it was funny.

But the rest of the report wasn't. First, they ran the footage of the Bike Barn and our yard on a loop along with some stills of the Rocky Shores Police Department while the reporter rattled on.

Police are examining other evidence, including security-camera footage from several area businesses. And in a Channel Seven exclu-sive, these are some rare images that a digi-tal camera sent to its owner's home computer via a memory card equipped with internet access.

Some photos came up on the screen. I squinted. "What is that? A living room full of bicycles?" I said.

Police believe that the camera was removed from the lost-and-found room at the Rocky Shores Police Department, where other valuables are also missing. They say that these incriminating images show the inside of Darren Macey's apartment. Meanwhile, Dewey Marriss and his four siblings say that none of them feel good about what hap-pened at the Bike Barn last night, but they are glad the thefts will stop.

"We did *not* say that," Lil said. She sounded disgusted. She picked up the remote and waited with her finger on the button.

The desk anchor said:

. . . and there may be good news coming along with those thunderstorms tonight. Please stay tuned this evening for the big story in national news, which surrounds some encouraging words from the newly formed National Department of Petroleum Trade and Distribution. Relief from the severe fuel crisis could be within sight . . .

Lil hit the button. The screen went blank.

"Hey," I said. "They were going to talk about fuel!"

"Talk, talk, talk. When it flows, we'll know about it."

I supposed she was right. "Well, at least it's true, what they reported," I said. "We *are* glad the thefts will stop."

"But that didn't come from us! They are fabricating!" Lil complained. "They just want to blow a little story up into a big one."

"Big news for little Rocky Shores," Vince said.

"Blah, blah . . . *unassuming little bike shop . . .*" Lil mocked and mumbled. She shook her head. "They're trying to create entertainment out of it." I couldn't understand why she felt so crabby about it.

The phone rang all through dinner. Everyone had seen the news. Everyone was in shock over the story of Officer Macey. We heard from Pop and Mattie. They wanted to come over but agreed with Lil that with the storm gathering it would be a terrible idea. Mrs. Bertalli sounded indignant on our behalf. We heard from a few of our regular milk-and-egg customers, and we took a couple of calls from people who had left bikes and wondered if they were safe. Finally, Robert called.

"It's crazy," he said. "It's like it happened right under everyone's noses." I was just happy to hear that Robert was feeling better and would come back in the morning.

The phone rang yet again. "Who else is left?" I said as I hopped up to grab the call. "Haven't we talked to everyone in town?" But it was Mom and Dad. They were calling in early. The connection was bubbly-sounding from the start. We cut through a lot of the is-everybody-okay talk. Mom was quick about saying that Runks had been keeping them apprised of the post–Bike Barn theft situation and that she and Dad were mightily sorry and fiercely proud of us. But she had something else to say—something important.

"Good news!" she cheered. The phone crackled. "We're on the move! That's why we're calling early. Not sure how the signal will be later on. We're getting into a line for diesel! They're supposed to get a delivery in the morning. Dad got a special stamp on his ration cards. It's a new process, but that's what the aid trucks are doing right now," she explained.

"Sounds like they're *rationing* the ration cards," I said.

Mom laughed. "You could say that. We've been told where to go. We aren't sure how many gallons they'll let us have, of course—"

"But you'll be able to at least *start* home?" I asked.

All four of my siblings' heads turned toward me then.

"Yes!" Mom said. "That's the idea! And I

cannot tell you how good that sounds."

It was the news we'd waited for. Yet it seemed to take its time to settle into my head now that it'd finally come. When Mom said good-bye, I stood still with the phone against my chest. This was it. The crunch was winding down. In my mind's eye I saw a gear turning and a pipe filling and slowly, slowly, a drop, then another and another until—

"*Dew!*" Lil shouted. She was staring at me.

"What?"

"What did they say?" Lil leaned toward me. "We heard something about starting home."

"Oh. Sorry," I said. "Yes! It's good news!" I announced that Mom and Dad were heading to a pump.

"Hah! I told you we'd hear about it if the fuel was really going to flow! But that was fast! There ya go!" Lil shouted. "Angus! Eva! Mom and Dad are about to get a fill-up!"

"W-well, they are getting in a line," I said. "And it seems like there will be at least *some* fuel."

"Oh," said Lil. "Okay, so it's maybe going to be a process . . ."

"So when will they get home?" Eva asked.

"We don't know yet," Lil said.

"But tomorrow. Maybe?" Angus suggested.

"They'll keep us posted," Lil said. "And we'll make another paper mural and you can draw the truck at all the stops it makes until it gets all the way home with Mom and Dad in it."

After that, the twins talked nonstop about Mom and Dad "getting gallons" at lots of pumps. They rolled out the butcher wrap and drew rows and rows of cars and trucks rolling along a crayon-stripe road.

"Did you tell Mom and Dad that we were on the news?" Lil asked. She drummed a finger on her bottom lip.

"Oh, I didn't even think of it," I said. I grinned. "Stardom. Easy come, easy go."

35

DARKNESS FILLED EVERY WINDOW. DISTANT rumbles moved closer and closer. I got up from the table and took a look outside.

"What do you see, Dew?" Lil called to me.

"The sky looks like seawater," I called back. "Churning up, green and gray. Has to rain. Has to."

It did. Soon we were into a full-fledged, crasher and banger of a summer thunderstorm. Lil got up and filled the sink. "So we have dish-washing water," she said. "I'm betting we lose power before it's over."

Crackle-crackle-BOOM! The house shook. *Crack-BOOM!* We answered with a chorus of *whoas!* and *wows!* Meanwhile, the rain began to pound our old dry roof.

"Rain! How long has it been?" Lil said.

"Before the Fourth of July," Vince said. A huge flash of lightning filled the windows.

"Before the gas pumps went dry!" I tried to get my words out before the next crash of thunder.

Cra-ck-crackle-CRACK . . . BOOM!

"Whoa! Close one!" Lil said.

"It's exciting!" said Eva. She gripped a crayon hard in her fist and wiggled side to side.

"I love it," said Angus.

"Me too," said Vince. He leaned back in his chair and stretched. But the next crash nearly sent him off his seat.

"Whoa! Wow!"

The lamp above our table flickered, then went out. (Lil is almost always right.) So there we were, lighting candles in the kitchen while the rain poured down.

After supper, we set the twins up at the sink for dish duty by candlelight. "Remember, the tap won't work when the power is out," I explained to Angus and Eva. "So wash in the warm and rinse in the cold."

"*And* what else?" Lil said. "What am I going to say?" She slid several plates into the sudsy water.

"Not too much soap," Angus answered.

"Right. And it's hard to see in here right now, so really watch how much is coming out."

I grabbed the broom. Vince grabbed the box of dog biscuits. He tucked it under one arm and began his game, leaping up to feed the dogs on the balcony. Every time he jumped he spilled several biscuits. I rounded them up with the broom and hockey-pucked them back to him.

"Ready! More dishes, please!" Eva called out.

"Vince will bring the dirty dishes from the table, won't you, Vince?" Lil said. She walked up to him and took the biscuit box from him. She set it on the table. "Easy with these," she said.

"Yeah, Goodie will make hisself puke!" Angus said.

Eva leaned up against the rim of the sink to look out the kitchen window. "It's still lightning out," she said.

"Eva, be careful," Lil warned. "Stay on your chair."

"Yeah," said Angus. "I see the yard every time—"

"A-a-hhhh!" Eva screamed. Then Angus screamed.

"What?" Lil hurried to be near them. "Tell me what!"

"Somebody is out there!"

"Oh no, Eva, don't fret," Lil said. She leaned toward the window. "Now, where? Where do you see someone?"

We all crowded at the window, waiting for another flash to light up the yard. Up on the balcony, Greatness started to bark. Goodness heard Greatness and joined in. They got more and more wound up. Collars jingled, toenails clicked. *Bark! Bark! Bark!*

"Hey, dogs!" I turned from the window. "Quiet! Quiet! Quie— Ahh!"

A hooded figure stood in our doorway.

I think all five of us screamed. Then we stopped.

The dripping body stepped into our kitchen.

The hood fell back and a hand shot forward.

"Mr. Spivey!" I gasped. He was already flinging and pecking with his crooked old finger. Surely he must be talking too. His mouth was moving.

The rain drummed. The thunder crashed. Goodness began to hack and gurgle. Greatness yapped. I could hear everything except our neighbor.

"Wait! I'm sorry. What are you saying?" I stepped closer to him.

"I say, it's gone down . . ." Fling and peck, fling and peck. ". . . fell on the fence out by the big one . . ." A roll of thunder covered his voice again.

I looked at Lil. Lil looked at me. I looked at Vince. None of us could keep from glancing up at the balcony where Goodness wretched and belched. No good would come. But we were all frozen in place. Sure enough, our old dog emptied his stomach right between the rungs of the railings. Vince looked at me wide-eyed. Lil must have seen it too.

"Uh, Mr. Spivey." She spoke very loudly. "Sorry—there's such a—a commotion. What are you saying? What's the trouble?"

Now Goodness began to nose at his lost meal. He pushed it closer and closer to the edge of the balcony.

"Uh-oh," said Angus. He covered his mouth with his hands and kept huge eyes fixed upward.

Mr. Spivey spoke again. "Tree's gone down . . . big one's climbed right up on the trunk. The brush cutter," he added, and he looked right at me when he said it. Suddenly I got what the old guy was saying.

"Oh! You're talking about *Sprocket*—"

Vince dove toward the table. He swiped up a dinner plate and lifted it high. I ducked. The dog puke landed in the center of the plate with a revolting splat.

"Ew!" said Eva.

"Didn't anybody hear me say 'uh-oh'?" said Angus.

Our neighbor looked at the plate, which Vince held sort of frozen in space. From above, the dogs mewed and tilted their heads. The Spive curled his lip and took a hard swallow. "Telling you . . . the tree went down—"

"The big pine fell?"

He nodded. "If that goat gets out—"

"Oh, holy! Vince, come on!" I grabbed a flashlight. We flew right past the Spive and out the door. We hopped the fence into the vegetable garden and ran between the rows until we reached the far pasture. The flashlight was no good, reflecting off every drop of rain. But in a flash of lightning we got our first look at the downed pine. A raw fissure in the trunk steamed. The scent of warm wood rose up. The tree had landed smack across the fence.

"See Sprocket anywhere?" I hollered to Vince.

"Naw!"

"Look at the tree! Destruction!"

I saw something move. Sprocket! One more flash of lightning and we saw the billy goat standing right up on the trunk of the tree. He looked over his shoulder at us through the draping boughs. A second flash, and we saw his pale, broad side heading down off the tree and out of the pasture. He was bound for the highway.

"*Spro-cket!*"

As if that goat would ever come when we called him.

"Hey! Hey!" Lil came charging toward us.

"Forget him!" she yelled. She circled one arm madly to gather us back home again. "You guys want to *die* out here? Notice the lightning?"

"It's passing. Besides, we had to try," I argued.

"Not in a storm, you *morons*!" she hollered. "God! Why not just carry your metal rods out here with you and point them toward the sky? Come on!" She turned and we followed.

The rain fell steadily on us all the way back to the house. As we neared the small barn we saw that the lights in the house had come back on. Then we heard the dinner bell—like an alarm.

"Oh no! Angus! Eva!" The three of us sprinted for the house.

Under the porch light we could see Eva pulling the bell cord.

"Lil-leey! Dew-eeey! Vince!" She called and called. She rang the bell again. "We ne-e-e-d you!"

I reached her first, took her in my arms. She looked at me with giant wide eyes all full of tears and said, "Dew-we-e-y, Angus is *bleeding*!"

"Oh, no, no, no!" I passed my little sister to Vince and rushed into the kitchen.

36

IT LOOKED BAD. A CHAIR HAD GONE OVER ON its side. Angus sat on the kitchen floor with his back against the cupboard. He had the neck of his T-shirt bunched up around his chin. When he let it drop it looked like he'd been stamped with a bib of blood.

"Oh, Angus!" Lil cried. "What did you do!" She rushed up to him and clamped his chin with a dishcloth.

"I sch-lipped," Angus said. Lil held his jaw still. But his lips quivered. "I usched too much schoap."

"Sorry!" Eva cried. "We both did it. And he leaned, and he slipped and he banged his chin on the counter going down. And he's ble-e-eding. . . ."

She clung to Vince, who rocked her calmly.

Lil eased her grip on the wound and we both went in for a closer look.

"Ish it gonna need schtitches?" Angus asked.

Lil said, "You know what? No." She looked at her dishcloth and seemed surprised and pleased. "This is okay," she said. "Check it out. It's not dripping blood."

"Uh . . . have you noticed . . . down the front of the shirt," Vince said.

"I know it," said Lil. "But I'm telling you, it's really a scrape. A good one. And a bruise coming. Can you open your mouth?" She coaxed Angus. She checked all his tiny teeth. "Not a single one is wiggly."

"And you didn't black out, or like, fall asleep, did you, Angus?" I thought I ought to ask.

Angus twisted up his face and told me, "No. I'm not asleep."

Lil sat back and let out a breath. "We are so lucky. So, so lucky."

We spent the next half hour or so bandaging up Angus. Talk about overkill. We darn near suffocated him with a four-handed effort involving antibiotic cream and every kind of Band-Aid in the box. We finished him off with an ice pack. We also exhausted him, which meant he and Eva went up to bed with no fuss.

Back down in the kitchen, Vince and I got out the mop and a bunch of rags. "No wonder he fell," I said as I rinsed the suds out of the mop and had yet another go at the floor.

"Soap slick," said Vince. He launched himself for a slide across the floor. He picked up the last plate from the kitchen table. "Ugh! The dog-puke plate!" he squawked, and gagged. He came sliding back to the sink, lost his footing, and nearly crashed. The two of us started to laugh.

"Hey! Cut it out!" Lil yelled. Top of her lungs.

Vince and I froze.

"Don't you get it?" she said. "Don't you know how lucky we got here tonight? And *no* thanks to you guys! Running out in a lightning storm. You imbeciles!" She swore. She was red and mad and teary.

I didn't really understand. I thought she was

being a little crazy. She'd said it herself: Angus was okay.

"Sorry," said Vince.

"Me too, Lil. I'm sorry." (Well, I didn't have to understand her to be sorry she was mad.)

"They are on their way home. *Finally!* Can we *just* hang on until then? *Can we?*" Her words rang loudly off the walls.

She was killing my ears.

"*That's it!*" she screamed. "That's *all* I'm ask-ing!"

"Okay!" I said. "Stop yelling!"

37

THE CHATTER WOKE ME. I OPENED MY eyes and stared at the ceiling beams above me. My ears filled with the sound of voices. I swung my legs out of bed and stood up. I leaned on the sill of the attic window and looked down.

Bikes. People. Puddles. Bikes, bikes, bikes, shining in the sun.

The line snaked across the yard. I craned my neck but could not see the end. A moan escaped from my gut. I staggered backward, sat on my bed, and grabbed my T-shirt up off the floor. For no particular reason, I balled it up, put it in my mouth, and bit down. Hard.

"What's going on?" Vince asked. He blinked.

I released my mouthful. "Look down in the yard."

He stumbled to the window and immediately drew back. He looked at me and gasped. "W-where does the line end?" he asked.

"Rhode Island."

"Not funny."

"I know. I'm calling Dad," I said.

"Talk to Lil first," Vince said. He covered his head with his pillow. "Don't wake me until all those people are gone."

I found Lil in her bed. She was already awake. "Did you see?" I said.

"No. But I can hear," she answered grimly. "This is all because of that damn news coverage."

"Oh. You're right." I hadn't thought of that. "I'm calling Dad," I said.

Dad picked up right away. He was almost always calm. But I heard a little edge in his voice that morning, and I'll bet it was because he heard a little edge in mine.

"D-dad, I didn't tell you because I didn't think much of it at the time . . . But there was this camera

253

crew here yesterday. And they put the Bike Barn on the news. Because of the theft."

Which I also didn't tell you about . . .

I got tangled up on the next part. "Dad, the customers—it's—lined up—uh . . ."

Dad waited for me. When I failed to cough out words he said, "You mean the Bike Barn has been fully *discovered*." I heard him sigh.

"Yes!" I started talking fast. "I think it's going to be too much. I-I can't ask Vince to face these people. The line goes down the driveway. We already have a lot of bikes. And we're so low on parts—"

"Tell you what, Dew," he said. "Are you dressed?"

"Uh, well, half," I said.

"Well, first thing is don't forget to put on your pants."

"Dad!"

"Well, I'm not kidding. That's important. Second is eat some breakfast, and while you're eating pretend that absolutely no one is out there. This is *your* time. And then you have to apply

Rule Eight: One problem at a time." He said this slowly. "It looks complex out there. But it's actually simple."

"Dad, the bikes are simple. The people are complex."

"Keep it about the bikes. That's your whole deal. People can be sweet, ornery, patient, or peevish, and it doesn't matter. Your response to them is all about the facts. If you don't have the part or you can't do the repair, that's all you have to say. If it's going to be several days, say so."

I thought for a second. I took a deep breath. "Okay," I said.

"Dew, call me anytime. And I'll check in, too. And is Robert coming to help today?"

"Yes! Oh, that's right! He *is* coming." I breathed a sigh of relief.

"So you'll have a third," Dad said. I think I heard him say "Phew!" just a bit under his breath.

"Hey, Dad? How did it go? Did you get to the station? Did you get fuel?"

"We got about half a tank just a half an hour ago," he said. "It's going to be tricky. I hope to make it to southern Maine on it today. But I have to keep calculating. And we'll need some good luck as well. Mom says the rig is our token and we're driving across a big game board," he said. "Advancing at the will of the rations." I could hear Dad smiling now. "You just have to make the most of it, Dew. Get on with your day. Go ahead. It'll work out."

"I'll start with my pants," I said, and Dad laughed out loud.

I spent the morning looking people in the eye. There was no time for anything but *bike facts* today. New mantra: It is all about the bikes.

"Could be hard to get this part," I told one guy. "It'll be at least five days before you hear from us. Maybe longer."

"Is this shop run by kids?" he asked.

"My father got stuck in the crunch. But we expect him home soon," I said. Facts, facts, facts.

Almost everyone took a chance and left their bikes with us. It was just too far to go limping to Sand Orchard or Centertown with a busted bike. We were *it*.

Robert arrived and he fell right in. He grabbed

a pen and some slips and started talking to people and logging bikes in. We passed each other pushing bikes to the paddock, and he said, "So do you think *anybody* on the planet missed that newscast? Because I don't."

"I think they broadcast our address," I joked. I wiped my forehead on my shirt and helped the next customer.

Angus and Eva decided to offer refreshments. They walked along the line of customers tugging our garden hose with them, saying, "Want a slurp?" and telling the tale of Angus's bandaged chin.

Lil came up to my ear and said, "Dewey, are you really logging in all these bikes? What did Dad say?"

I was way too busy to talk to her. "Yeah. He said we'll work it out. But I'm telling people—Robert and I are both being clear—that it'll probably be a while. Hey, Lil, the twins can be out here. But I can't *watch* them," I said. "I really can't."

Lil looked down the line of customers. She nodded to me. "Maybe I'll just take them down to the beach today."

By late morning the yard was clear enough that Vince came out of hiding. He and Robert and I worked nonstop until three o'clock, when all of us simultaneously and absolutely had to stop and eat a bunch of food and drink a few gallons of water. But after that we went back out for one last push.

"This is the best job I have ever had." Robert stuck another finished order on the call spindle. "*So* satisfying!"

"You'll learn to despise it," Vince told him. But Robert just laughed.

Truth was, Robert was just the dose of energy that the Bike Barn needed. And he was an adult. Good for our image, I thought. We were finally locking up the shop when a sunburned Angus— back from the beach—came running with the phone. "For you, Dewey," he said.

"Young Mr. Marriss?"

"Mr. Bocci? Is that you?" I strolled toward the house as I talked.

"Yes-yes. I called to see how you are doing. I saw that news report. Who could guess about a bad cop? Terrible. Terrible."

"Who could guess that helping catch him would make our lives this crazy?" I said.

"Is it about the business? What you are saying?"

"Well, yes. As my dad said, we've been *discovered*."

"Yes. All the publicity you never wanted, hey?"

"I guess so. Yes. That's right. We are so small. Th-there needs to be more of us," I said. "I mean, more bike shops."

"Anything I can do to help, you call me," Mr. Bocci said.

I *knew* we needed parts. But I didn't know which ones—not right there and then. It'd been such a hectic day. I hadn't read all the slips and hadn't taken time to check my parts inventory. I didn't want to admit it.

"I-I'm set, Mr. Bocci. Doing fine. Thanks so much," I said.

38

"STOP CLAWING AT THAT BANDAGE, ANGUS," Lil warned.

"So, wait," he was saying, "my sunburn is going to turn to a tan, right? And then when I take the bandage off I'm going to look like I have a beard?"

"That's right." Vince was teasing him. "A white one."

"Cool."

"If it was me, I could be a bearded lady-girl," Eva said.

My siblings kept laughing and talking at the picnic table. I was spacey. Tired. Thinking. And suddenly, I was listening, though not to them.

"Earth to Dew. What's the matter with you?" Lil gave me a nudge.

"Shh!" I turned around on the picnic bench. I waited and listened some more. "Do you hear that?" I asked. We waited.

"I just hear the quiet," Eva said.

"I hear . . . the highway," I said. "It's trucks. I swear." I stood up. "I'm going to see."

"Take me, Dewey!" Eva came running.

"Report back!" Lil called. "I can't *wait*!"

I swung Eva up onto my back and jogged out our driveway and past the trees. We broke into the open at Bridal Path Lane—the on-ramp—and waited. All was quiet.

"Dew, I don't see trucks," Eva whispered. "Just bikes."

"But see where the bikes are? See how they're all keeping to the right side? They're leaving room," I said.

By now Vince had come up behind us with Angus, who ran up and wrapped himself around one of my legs. "Where's the trucks?" he asked.

"Shh! Listen! Watch!" I said. We all stared out at the highway to the north. "Hold on. Something's coming. It's coming. . . ."

"Truck!" cried Angus.

"Yes! See! And look behind it. And one more after that."

"Convoy!" Vince cheered.

That was a stretch. This barely qualified as *traffic*. Sometimes there were several minutes between rigs. But it still felt historic. We walked to the wedge of grass that split the highway from the ramp and stood watching the trucks pass. The back drafts sucked at our clothing. The brush and brown grasses bent, then popped up again. We took to waving at the drivers. They honked their horns.

"Dad will honk," Eva said. "He'll honk all the way home!"

Highway biking would come to an end, I realized. In fact, I was sure it was already over for those of us who had Lilly Marriss calling the shots. She'd never let us out here now. A tiny seed of regret settled in my chest. We hadn't taken enough advantage of the empty highway. Not as riders. But I smiled to myself when I thought about how many bikers we'd put out there with all our repairs. And more to go . . .

We watched a few more sets of headlights come

over the horizon. They seemed like the winking-blinking proof, somehow, that Mom and Dad would be home soon. Bedtime caught up to Angus and Eva. Soon they were just staring. I'd watched them do this before—reach the end of the day with their eyes still open but with everything else all gone to sleep. They would not speak any more now. How good it must feel, I thought.

"Let's go back," I whispered to Vince. "I don't want to miss the call tonight. I want Dad to know we made it through the day. In fact, I'm surprised he hasn't called. It's late."

I lifted Eva to my shoulder, and Vince took Angus.

We heard the phone ringing from the porch step. Lil answered it as we walked inside.

"Hello? Mom? You guys are calling late! Angus and Eva are"—she looked at our cargo—"already asleep." She covered the phone and whispered to me, "Did you see trucks?" I nodded, and she made a huge grin with her eyes closed. She waved Vince and me on up the stairs. She turned back to the receiver and said, "Mom? Okay, tell me."

Upstairs, Vince and I each slid an unconscious

twin onto their beds. "They're dirty," Vince whispered. He picked up one of Angus's limp feet and examined the grime. "We should try to wash them again before Mom and Dad get here."

"Yeah," I said. "Except, my fantasy is that Mom and Dad have a full tank. And they're driving through the night to surprise us."

When we got back downstairs, Lil was facing the kitchen window, her back to us. Her fingers were still around the handset of the phone. She suddenly picked it up and gave it two hard slams on the countertop then pushed it to the floor. She grabbed a dish towel and stood with it pressed tight to her eyes. I saw her back convulse. My sister was sobbing.

"Lil?" I said. "Lil, what's happening?"

She drew a breath inward, made a high-pitched sound like nothing I had ever heard come from Lil before. She swallowed hard, wiped her face, and said, "Dad's been hurt."

"Hurt? How? A crash?"

"Somebody *attacked* him." She choked again. "And they did it for those—*goddamn ration cards*. Oh my God. You guys." She looked at us almost as if *we* were giving her the news instead of the other way around. "Someone *beat* our dad and they *robbed* him. For *fuel*."

Vince grabbed his head with his hands and said, "No!"

I was frozen where I stood, but I could feel my heart falling.

Beaten and robbed? What does that even mean? I needed to know. Couldn't ask. Dad is one of the nicest people on the planet. He'd sooner give you a ration card . . .

"How—how bad is it?" I said. "How bad is Dad?"

"Mom said—he—has a concussion. Stitches over one eye. And his hand is badly hurt. Broken, they think."

"Oh my God."

"He's—he's going to recover," Lil said. She shook her head quickly. "I—I should have said that. Sorry." She took a new breath and said, "But with the head injury, they're keeping him in the hospital. At least a few nights."

My own head felt light. I let myself into a chair at our kitchen table. I wanted to talk to Dad. I had never wanted anything more.

39

FOR THE SECOND NIGHT IN A ROW, I DIDN'T SLEEP much. I thought about Dad half the night and about all the bikes in the Bike Barn the other half. When I got upset about Dad's injuries I could at least remember Lil's words. *He's going to recover.* I'd relax and think I was going to fall asleep. But when it came to the backlog of bikes, there was no relief. For days I'd been telling myself that everything would be okay *when Dad got home*. But I had to face two things. One, Dad wouldn't be able to drive for a while. Mom didn't have a commercial license. Two, it would be pretty tough for Dad to repair bikes with a busted hand.

So after greasing my brain on those thoughts all night long, I finally dozed off for an hour or so right around sunrise. When I woke, I rubbed my face and looked out the window. The yard was full of broken bikes and owners. Again. I stumbled down the stairs.

"No! No! Please don't come to the house!" I heard Robert say as he came up our steps. He was speaking to the swarm. "Just line up. Yep. Just like you are. The barn is where the business is." From the window I saw him point his arm straight and hard at the building as if to direct them away from our house. Smart, I thought. He came inside and we shut the door together.

"Ai-yi-yi," he muttered. "I thought they were going to follow me in. I left my bike around back of the house. Too many envious looks!" He set a bag of bagels on the table. Then he faced me. "Hey," he said, "you okay? You look wiped out, Boss Man. Oh, gosh, I didn't give you that stomach bug, did I?"

"Nope." My voice croaked. "We had a bad night."

"What happened?" Robert asked. "No more thefts . . . oh, no! Don't tell me . . ."

I shook my head no. I told him about Dad.

"Oh, you *cannot* be telling me this," Robert

said. He settled himself on the edge of our kitchen table. Turned his palms up. "W-hat can I do?"

"You can't do anything," Lil said. Boy, did she sound like she was at the wrong end of the day. No morning cheer. She held out a pair of Eva's shorts to me. "Dew, Eva's being a snot. Take these up and wrestle her into them. And get Angus and Vince moving too. And don't forget to get dressed yourself," she added.

I shot her a look. So what, I had come down in my boxers and a T-shirt. I didn't need to be told to get dressed. Especially not in front of Robert.

"I want us all together when I sit the twins down and tell them about—" She cut herself off. Stood looking at Robert.

"Dewey told me about your dad. I'm so sorry," Robert said. "Look, I came to work in the shop, but how can I really help the most?"

Lil didn't answer him. She flapped Eva's shorts at me impatiently. "Take these. Please?" she said.

I told Robert I'd be right back. "We'll eat and then go face the mob together."

"You got it, Boss Man," he said, and I saw Lil wince like she had a bumblebee up her nose.

I ran the stairs two at a time. Maybe Lil would be nice to Robert long enough that they'd get some of those bagels toasted. The smell would get everyone into the kitchen.

I passed the attic stairwell and called up to Vince. "Get up! The yard is full again!" I banged the wall with the flat of my hand.

He called back. "I. Don't. Care."

I stood still with my teeth gritted and my fists balled up, but only for a second. "At least I have Robert," I mumbled to myself. I turned the corner into Angus and Eva's room. Eva immediately went into a fit about the shorts—*not* what she wanted to wear that day. She flung them to the floor. Angus sat up and began pawing at the bandage on his chin. I cautioned him—too harshly, I guess, because he started to melt down.

Time to be firm.

"Angus, chill out. Eva, you get dressed."

"No, *you* get dressed." She showed me her bottom lip.

We struggled a bit more. I felt bad. We usually didn't butt heads like this. It was a relief to finally march them both into the bathroom to wash up.

Meanwhile, I picked up an armload of dirty clothes off their floor and headed for the hamper in our back hall. I banged my toe—something wicked—on the baseboard.

"Ow!" I grabbed the toe and squeezed it hard. "And doesn't *that* just have to happen today?" I hopped and groaned.

The hamper was overflowing, so I started to split the lights and darks as fast as I could. It was a job that messed with me because Lil always corrected the piles anyway.

"You did too get it in my hair!" I heard Eva wail from the bathroom.

"No, you did it yourself! My toothpaste is on my own brush. See!"

"Ouch! Now you scratched my arm, didn't you? Angus!"

"Where?"

"Right there! See the marks? You *toothbrushed* me!"

"No . . ."

"Angus! Eva!" I boomed from the hallway. "Cut it out in there. Get the job done!"

It was going to be a hard day. They were already crabby, and we still had to break the news about Dad. *And* there were all those customers in the yard and bikes in the barn. *And* we lacked parts to fix half of them—okay, okay. This was not positive thinking. What would Dad be saying about today?

Take time for yourself in the morning.

Breakfast. Bagels! Fresh bagels! Bagels to make everyone happy. That was a bright spot to this morning. And all because of Robert, who had come to us in the first place all because of *bikes*. Yes. The universe is connected!

Robert was my godsend!

That's when I heard Lil's voice coming up from the backyard, and boy, did she sound serious.

"Look, I know you're older than I am, Robert. I know you are an adult. But this is my family, and I've been left in charge. Could you please just respect me here? This is a tough decision. I think it's better if you aren't here when I tell him."

Robert sounded desperate. "There must be something I can do to help even if—"

"I just need you to leave."

Leave? Oh, no, no! You can't send the god-send away!

"Well," said Robert. "Okay then."

I heard a pedal set rotate backward. He was getting on his bike!

I hollered. "No!" I darted down the hall and swung myself around the banister. I thundered down the stairs. I wove past Goodness and Greatness, who tried to corral me for a greeting, and went tripping over them to the rear door.

By the time I reached the backyard, Robert was out of sight. Lil looked at me wide-eyed.

"Uh, Dewey, listen. Robert is gone."

"Yeah," I said. "I heard. *What were you thinking, Lil?* Ever heard of strength in numbers?" I glared at her. "Have you forgotten that the brother upstairs in the attic is people *phobic*? What am I supposed to do now? I *want* Robert here. I need him here!"

"Dewey, I'm sorry." She fixed her eyes on me. "I'm *not* going to let you log in any more bikes," she said. "I sent Robert away because he's a part of the Bike Barn, and the Bike Barn *has to stop*."

"*Stop?* Oh, Lil!" I wailed. "Seen the crowd out front? It's not going to stop!" I pointed a finger at her and said, "You're trying to make me fail!"

"Dewey, that's not fair—"

"Not fair? I'll tell you what's not fair. All those people out there with busted bikes," I said. "Not fair is me trying to handle every last one of them alone. It's not fair that I have to *protect* Vince. It's not fair that there's no one else who can put those people back on the road—"

"Dewey!" Lil stared at me. She got so calm it was maddening. She leaned toward me. "*I'm sorry. I should have stepped up sooner. I knew it was too many bikes—*"

"The Bike Barn is *me*, Lil! My job!"

"But the crunch made it too big." She shook her head. She gave me a look I hated—a pitying sort of face. "You can't do it alone, Dewey. You can't."

"Hah!" I shouted. "You sent my help away, and now you tell me I can't do it alone!" I stood there, breathing at her through my nose. "You want to shut me down, Lil? Forget it! I'll do it myself!"

I marched around the house into the front yard and hollered, "Go!" So many pairs of eyes stared back.

"Oh no! Hey, buddy, we've been waiting since—"

"I'm *closed*!" I cried. "Closed, closed, closed. No more repairs."

The mob spoke. Their sentences blurred.

Just look at my shifter cables—I've got to get to—I can't move the seat post—it's a simple flat— I'll pay you double—I just have a broken chain— lost my Allen wrench—will you sell me—can I use your—there is no place else to go . . .

I stood there shaking my head. "No," I said. "None of you know. Ev—everybody wants bikes. We've been alone. My—my father can't come home—"

"Dew." It was Lil with her hand on my shoulder. I was on auto-rant.

"We're just a tiny shop. W-we were never supposed to be this big."

"Dew," Lil said again, "you don't have to explain."

The hot morning fell quiet except for a nanny goat bleating in the distance. Then a tiny bit of birdsong. The low murmur of hens. The heat ringed my nostrils. Choked my throat.

"Sorry, everyone. Sorry to turn you away," Lil said. She sounded sweet. Like another bird chirping in the yard. "We need you to leave."

There were groans and mutters. People turned their crippled bikes and began to slowly roll them away. Lil ushered them along, keeping up her apologetic song.

I stood by. Numb. Mute.

I think everyone was gone when I finally turned and started up the steps into the house. I watched my bare feet—the newly swollen toe—my bare knees—the hem of my boxers.

My boxers.

On top of everything else, I had gone outdoors without my pants.

40

BREAKFAST WAS EXCRUCIATING. HARD TO SIT AT the table with Lil. Hard to face our ornery twins knowing we had nothing but bad news for them. It was the last place I wanted to be. But mad as I was at Lil, I wouldn't leave it on her to tell them.

We held Angus and Eva in our arms. There were lots of tears that morning. We passed them from lap to lap to try to comfort them. They were full of questions:

Did the bad guy punch Dad? What about everybody else who has those ration cards? Could the bad guys hurt everybody? Did the truck break? Can Dad still drive it?

Everything was so hard to answer.

But when it came to Dad's injuries, Angus had

his own answer, even as tears streamed down his face. He said, "I don't know about that concussion, but if Dad got banged up like my chin . . ." He tapped his bandage. "Well, it's okay. It gets better."

"Yes, and Dad *will* recover," Lil repeated. "And there is fuel and they will get home. We just have to wait. Some more."

It was Vince who moved us along that day. He got up from the table, picked up his milk buckets, and called for Angus and Eva to come with the egg baskets. "Chores to do," he said. "Just like yesterday." He sent them out the door in front of him. Then he turned back to me.

"I thought you said the yard was full of customers again this morning. Did I dream that?" I couldn't believe he'd missed the firestorm in the front yard—me shouting at Lil and going crazy. In my underwear.

"No. You *nightmared* it," I said.

"Huh?"

Lil covered. "Dewey told them that we couldn't take any more bikes," she said.

Half a story, but I let it go.

"Really?" Vince looked surprised. "So we'll just knock off jobs when we feel like it?" His buckets clanked against the doorjamb.

"Whatever," I said. "Take the whole day off if you want."

When Vince was good and gone, Lil spoke. "Look, I know you blame me—"

"*Did* someone else send Robert away?" I asked.

"No." Lil sat down across from me. She folded her arms across her chest. "I did that. But don't think that I liked it. Dewey, you were like this machine taking in bikes. You wouldn't stop! I had to shut you down, and I didn't want to embarrass you by doing it in front of Robert."

"Yeah. I like it lots better when you go behind my back," I said. We endured a beat of silence. "I wanted him here," I said. "It's not just that he's a good mechanic, either."

"What do you mean?"

"Look, I get it. Mom and Dad *cannot* come home. I'm no baby. And it's nothing against you, Lil, but I liked just having that extra adult around." I thought for a second. "It's not even all about Robert. I like it when Pop and Mattie touch base. Or when Runks rides up. You're so busy telling everyone we don't need anything. But Lil, I'm half-glad knowing that *the Spive* is next door! Can you believe that?"

"Last part kind of surprises me," she said. "But I get the rest. If you want, we'll have another dinner in the yard. Whatever." She paused and said, "But ask yourself, aren't you just a little bit relieved that the yard isn't full of strangers, that you're not logging in more bikes today? That you don't have to decide—"

I shoved back my chair. "Don't *be the parents* on me, Lil."

I went upstairs and put on my pants. When I came back down, I sailed straight out the door without looking at her. I went out to the barn and I stood around in the open doorway to the shop. Angus and Eva came out of the coop with baskets of eggs while both dogs and the Athletes followed. They looked busy.

"You guys okay?" I asked.

"Yeah. We just really, really want Dad to be all right," said Eva. "So we're planning a surprise for him."

"What's that?" I asked.

Angus whispered, "We're going to get rid of our thief." He pointed to Mr. Spivey's yard.

"Once and for all," said Eva, and she gave me a devilish grin.

"Whoa, whoa, whoa," I said. "What's the plan? You better tell me."

"Well . . . we're going to sneak. And we're going to put a carton of eggs by his door every week. If he already has eggs, then he won't need to steal anymore. And he won't be a thief."

"Oh . . ." I said. "You know what? That will work. Brilliant plan."

Eva nodded. "I know," she said. She turned back to Angus and said, "How about if it's like a birthday card? 'To Mr. Spivey,'" she recited, "'Eggs for you . . . Happy Breakfast to you.' And that's all."

So now a gift for the Spive. I shook my head. What a morning. I dragged out an old barn board.

I took some of Lil's famous blue paint (without asking) and I made a sign: BIKE BARN CLOSED. I leaned the sign up against a couple of cedars at the end of the driveway and pressed back the weeds so nobody would miss it.

I plugged along with the jobs we had already logged in, but more by rote than by drive now. I felt like a guy who had forgotten how to do anything but fix bikes. Not so, Vince. He took his fishing pole and went for a bike ride. He showed up again early afternoon to take a tough job or two.

"Do you know if there's been any word from Mom today?" I asked.

"Yeah," he said. "Dad's less groggy. Talking. Apparently a lot."

"Is he? Oh, good." Truth was, I wanted to phone him.

"I guess they're having trouble making him rest."

"That sounds like Dad. How was your ride?"

"Good. I watched the highway from the overpass. A few more trucks around. Still pretty quiet out there. Change didn't come overnight. Oh, and

281

wanna hear something funny?"

"Yeah."

"I saw Sprocket."

"No!" I set down a wrench. Looked at my brother.

"He's doing community service. Taking down the weeds by the exit sign. Making himself right at home. He saw me. Moved off into the brush, the brat."

"Shoot. So he's hanging out by the highway. And now the trucks are moving. I bet he'd walk into traffic just to spite me."

"Naw. He won't jump the guardrail, and if he does, he takes his life in his own hands—hooves," said Vince.

"It never pays to chase him," I conceded.

"Stubborn. But he'll come home on his own." Vince swirled grease off his finger onto the seat post of a BMX bike he'd been working on. It'd come in for a wheel repair. But we often covered Rule Three as a courtesy: An ounce of maintenance is worth a pound of repairs. He worked the seat post into the tube. He tightened the screw and said, "There. Another one ready to ship out." He rolled the bike forward and stuck the order on the call spindle. "You did a lot today," he said. It was true. The spindle had about seven finished jobs on it. "So when do we take in more?" he asked.

"No more," I said. I surprised myself.

"What? You're kidding?"

"Nope. I want to clear the Bike Barn."

"Then what?"

"Then I don't know," I said. "But I can't see Dad coming home to this. Especially with a busted hand. I don't even want him to see the mess I've made."

41

WE ALL THOUGHT IT'D BE MOM WHEN THE phone rang during supper that night. But Lil handed it to me.

"Young Mr. Marriss?" It was Mr. Bocci again. "My team went by your exit today. They saw your sign. You closed up shop?"

"Yes, sir," I said. I took a tough swallow. "Not taking any more in." I set my fork down in my eggs and glanced up at Vince. He gave me a shrug.

"Is this about you needing parts?" he asked. "I can help you some."

"Oh, thank you. Parts are—well, parts are only part of it," I said.

"Yah!" He laughed. I guess he felt I was playing with my words.

"We've had some more bad luck," I said, and I went on to tell him about what had happened to Dad. "He'll be okay," I started to say. But Mr. Bocci got excited. He was loud and spoke fast. I held the receiver away from my ear.

"Ah! The gas begins again and then somebody *beats* this man? This good *father* so they can have some card so they can get precious, precious gasoline! Terrible, terrible!" he said. "What has it come to?"

"I guess it's gotten nasty out there," I said, though I hated to use the words. "Anyway, the Bike Barn is taking a break." My face ached in that about-to-start-crying sort of way. I always fight that feeling and it always gets worse.

"You sound low of spirit," Mr. Bocci said.

"Umm. Well. Somewhat," I said. Now I was having trouble speaking.

"Well, you need something, you can call me. Maybe I'll have the team stop by? You can give them a list. You want this?"

Sure, send Team Bocci over to see the collapsing little bike shop. . . .

"W-we're okay." I squirmed. "Thanks. Thanks so much, Mr. Bocci."

After I hung up I felt miserable *and* stupid. *Of course* I needed parts.

Especially if I wanted to clear bikes.

Just an hour or so after Mr. Bocci called, the phone rang again. Again, Lil held it out to me. "Dewey, Dad wants to talk to you."

My hand was thick and clumsy on the receiver— like if I held it too tightly, I'd somehow be hurting Dad. "Dad? Hi." I spoke softly.

"Oh heck, am I going deaf on top of everything else? Dewey? You there? I can hardly hear you."

I laughed. "No, Dad, sorry. I just thought I should keep it down since you're in the hospital. Dad, how are you?"

"Feel like I went a few rounds with something large and unintelligent," he said. "And I'm not very pretty. They've got my eye stitched up like a baseball and my hand looks like a boiled lobster claw."

"Dad, it's horrible," I said. "Horrible somebody did this to you."

"It is what it is, Dewey. It's the times. Listen,

I'm going to be fine," he said. "I've got everybody taking care of me here. What about you, Dew?" He was more serious now. "I hear the shop's been tough."

I knew he must have heard that from Lil. "I—I'm trying to work it out," I said. I cleared my throat. "It got so busy. We had to stop taking bikes in."

"Ran out of room, did you?"

"You could say." I wondered how much Lil had told him. Hardly mattered. I wasn't about to bother Dad with a sibling fight. "I'm tired," I finally said.

"Well, you should be! All you've done! Dewey, I'm so proud. And as for right now, well, it's easy for me to say it from here, sitting on my butt in a hospital bed, but all problems have an answer."

"Yeah, I keep trying to figure out which of our Eight Rules That Apply to Fixing Almost Anything applies to fixing this," I said.

"Have you tried turning the whole Bike Barn clockwise?"

I laughed. "Well, 'one problem at a time' worked for a while. But the whole thing's come disassembled now. Dad, you might have to just tell me what the answer is this time," I joked, but in the most hopeful way.

"I wish I knew," Dad said. "I've never seen it like you're seeing it. But I'll listen to you talk it out."

I repeated what I had already said in the past. "There are just *so* many." I told Dad that the repairs were simple. "In fact, if they were harder— way above my head—it'd be easier to turn them away. But there's not much I can't do. And almost *nothing* Vince can't do," I said. "So, I've taken in all these jobs, and I guess I have too many now. And then there's the problem of getting parts."

Dad was calm and kind. "There's nothing to be done about parts. That's happening with everything all across the country right now—and not just in the bike business. But, Dew, I swear, some kind of answer is probably right in front of you. It's somehow there with the bikes, or maybe even with the people."

"The people?" I said. "Okay, now you sound like a guy who got hit in the head," I said.

Dad laughed. "Hey, I'm sorry. Your mom's here nagging me to wrap it up and get some rest."

"Okay, Dad. You should do that. I'll—I'll work on this," I told him.

"Or maybe *don't* work on it. Maybe better to relax and *let* it come."

Let it come.

I could not for the life of me think what that meant.

42

IT IS A CLICHÉ TO SIT BOLT-UPRIGHT IN BED IN the middle of the night when an idea strikes. But that's exactly what I did.

I'd been *not sleeping* while I replayed my conversation with Dad.

Somewhere right around two o'clock in the morning I started repeating three things to myself over and over again:

The bikes. The Eight Rules for repairing them. The people.

Something was coming to me. I wasn't sure what. I needed a genius.

"Psst! Vince? Psst!"

My brother moved in his bed. Slightly.

"Hey, Vince. Psst! Psst! *Ps-s-st!*"

"Wha-what?" Vince sat up, just halfway.

"You awake?"

"What?" He squinted at our clock. "No," he decided, "I'm not."

"I need your help. I'm trying to think."

"Well, do it with your own brain," he complained. He threw himself facedown into his pillow.

"Feed me the Eight Rules," I said.

Vince groaned.

"Come on. One at a time," I said.

He spoke into his pillow. "Wule Wun: Wight ish tight."

"Right is tight. Probably the simplest rule. Okay. Go again," I said.

Vince rolled faceup. He sighed. "Rule Two: Proper tools."

"Yes . . ." Hadn't someone even asked to borrow something? Someone in that crowd of customers that I'd turned away? "Proper tools if you have them," I said. "And we do. But most of the people who come to the shop don't."

"Profound," said Vince. He went on to Rule Three robotically. "An ounce of maintenance is worth a pound of repairs."

I settled onto my back again and thought out loud. "If people knew how to do a few simple things for their bikes, we'd never even see them. . . ."

"Rule Four." Vince yawned. "Rust never sleeps. And neither does my brother."

"Hmm. Tightly tied to Rule Three," I said. "Okay, next one."

"Rule Five: Study the problem."

"Or . . ." I thought for a second. "Find someone to explain it to you."

"Rule Six." (He was pretty much cutting me off now.) "Try the least expensive fix first."

"But if you have to hire someone, that adds to the expense."

"Eh . . . well . . ." Vince stopped and thought. "Not so sure about that," he said. "Sometimes it pays to go with a pro."

"Right. Or consult one . . . Okay, give me Seven."

"Take notes on complicated jobs."

I flashed on the cheat sheets that Dad had made for us when we first started to do repairs—the ones that Robert had been looking at so recently.

"How to proceed," I said.

"Rule Eight: My nightmare. One repair at a time; don't disassemble more than you have to. Goes with knowing when to get help from a pro," he added, and he yawned again, loudly.

I knew what he meant. People brought us bikes that they'd tried to fix by themselves all the time. "Components in pieces," I said.

"Yes-s-s . . . but, of course, Dad has a soft spot for do-it-yourselfers," Vince said, and he let out one small laugh.

"Yeah. That's Dad. Always willing to help them."

Help. Them.

Then Dad's words echoed.

Let. It. Come.

Let them come.

In the dark of the attic bedroom, I   said one word straight into the hot summer night.

"Clinic."

It was more than a word; it was a decision. I got out of bed.

"Dew?"

"Sleep, Vince. Sleep for both us," I said.

I went downstairs to the computer. That's where Lil found me maybe an hour later.

"Dewey!" she whispered. "It's the middle of the night."

"Leave me alone," I said.

"That's pretty snotty." She hovered behind me.

"Okay. Sorry. Leave me alone, *please*. I'm hatching a plan."

"Oh, that can't be good," she tried to joke, but I wasn't having it.

"Go back to bed, Lil."

"Hey, who do you think you are?"

"Still the temporary manager of the Bike Barn," I said. "Good night, Lil."

43

"'PUT THE MARRISS BIKE BARN OUT OF Business'?" Vince read as sheets of paper came breezing out of the printer.

"It's a joke. Sort of," I said. I was bouncing around. Energy to burn. "It's an attention grabber, don't you think?"

Vince shifted his weight. Arched his eyebrows. "Hmm. Guess so . . ." He started to read on. I grabbed the page away from him.

"Now listen up," I told my siblings. "This is a lot to take in before breakfast, but this is what we're doing. And I need everyone."

The twins stared. Lil nodded slightly—all her focus on me.

"Here it is." I showed them. "It's a self-help

bike clinic," I said. "It's tomorrow—all day long. And it's free."

"Free," Lil repeated.

"Yep. Because Dad is hurt. And he can't come home to all those bikes. We need to at least reduce 'em way down. That's my goal. People can pay for parts. If we even have them." I tried not to sound miserable about that. "I'm calling Pop and Mattie. We'll get Runks, too, if we're lucky."

"But Dew, Pop and Mattie aren't bike mechanics," Lil broke this news to me gently.

"But they can help," I said, and I tilted my head toward the twins. "We're going to be busy. We'll need all kinds of help. And Pop will be good with crowd control if we need him."

"Cr-rowd," Vince said. His jaw hung.

"I have a plan," I said. "I'm going to hide you in the loft. Cord across the stairs. Limited access to the genius. You'll be all set up and you can do one-on-ones for the complicated jobs. The customer becomes your assistant."

"You're going to take care of all the rest? By yourself?"

"*Self-help,*" I said. "I know, I know. It's going

to be hard to pull this off, but I made these." I grabbed a stack of papers off the desk and fanned them. "I typed up copies of—"

"Dad's cheat sheets," Vince said.

"We'll set up stations with the right tools and instructions for these basic jobs. Seventy-five percent of our work is simple stuff that people could do with a little guidance and—"

"Proper tools," Vince finished my sentence again.

"It's going to be heck," I said. "Even hell. But people want their bikes. They are motivated. And if it clears even *some* bikes out of the barn, I'm all about it."

Meanwhile, Lil was reading over my flyer. She finished and tapped the corner of the page against her bottom lip. "One thought," she said. "Why put this out there? Why not limit it to the bikes you already have logged in? You have all the phone numbers."

"Two reasons," I said. (It was good to be the guy with all the answers.) "First, not everyone will come. Not everyone will want a self-help clinic. And second, I feel bad about yesterday. About the people I sent away. It was the things they said that gave me this idea. Maybe some of them will see the signs and come back. I would feel good about that."

"O-kay . . ." Lil said. She was not convinced. "So here's another thought," she said. "You're right, this is catchy wording—'put the Bike Barn out of business.' It's cute. But . . ."

"I'm not taking any buts," I said.

"Your decision. But I suggest you use FREE BIKE CLINIC as your first line. In bigger letters."

"I'll run out of space. Besides, it says 'free clinic' farther down."

"Nothing wrong with mentioning that it's free twice," she said. She thought for a second. "And people will feel more *patient* because it is free. *They'll be nicer.*" She put on a big smile. "So drive that home, Dew. Keep these. Just print it separately—real big—and we'll put the two pages up together." She looked me in the eye. "That's the idea, right? Put this up around town?"

"Yes. On the Post Road. And definitely out at the end of our own drive. We'll plaster them over the bummer sign I put out yesterday."

"Okay," Lil said. "I'll take Angus and Eva and we'll do that while you and Vince set up here."

"And one last thing, Lil." I squared up my shoulders. "I'm hiring Robert back. I need at least one other person who knows what he's doing. You *have* to say yes," I told her. "You have to."

She nodded slowly. "Makes sense," she said.

Yes! I had Lil. That meant I had them all.

44

EARLY THE NEXT MORNING, POP AND MATTIE arrived with the sun. Runks switched his shift to join us for the day. He stood in the kitchen singing, "Oh, What a Beautiful Morning" at the top of his lungs. Only he was changing the lyrics.

"'There's a bright golden haze on the Bike Barn . . .'"

"*Meadow!*" The twins laughed and tried to correct him. He sang straight over them. "There's a bright golden haze on the Bike Barn . . . The orders are high as an astronaut's eye . . ."

". . . and Miss Gloria Cloud just pinched a fresh pie . . ." Robert drowned out Runks as he made his entrance.

We groaned. Then we laughed.

"Ah! But she's a crowd pleaser," said Robert.

"You've got takers," he said. "People in the yard."

Lil surprised me. She was cheery. "Good morning, everybody! Thanks *so* much for coming to help."

You would have thought we were about to throw a party. And why not? Why not at least try to think that way? Who knew what the day would bring? This was an experiment.

"Okay, everyone, we have the next twelve minutes for ourselves. Everyone knows what they're doing. So for now, pretend there is no one out there," I said. Of course, I looked out the window immediately. I saw about eighteen people bringing bikes and probably just as many arriving solo. I figured they had come to work on bikes that were already logged in. I'd done a lot of phoning the day before. Of course, once we saw the crowd, neither Vince nor I could eat. I was excited. He was stricken.

Runks came up beside me. "Dewey, I am *quite* certain this belongs to you," he said. He was slipping something into my hand.

"What?" I looked down at a roll of cash.

"Among the items in Macey's apartment," he said. Then he added, "Smell it."

I did. Peppermint.

"Thank you," I said. I closed my fingers around the roll. "And for keeping it on the down low, too."

Runks pulled us together for a good-luck hum, as he called it. "Something my theater group does before opening night," he explained. We joined hands and sent a vibe through the kitchen that made Greatness howl and prance, while poor deaf Goodness just tilted his head at us. When the buzz was gone, we lined up to go outside. "Everyone ready?" I asked.

Angus and Eva began to march in place.

Pop Chilly raised his thermos of iced coffee and hollered, "Cheers!"

Mattie said, "May the mob prove gracious!"

"Hear! Hear!" cried Runks. "Oh, and to assist you, Dewey . . ." He pulled a megaphone out of a duffel bag. "Courtesy of the Rocky Shores PD!" He leaned toward me and said, "We owe you that much."

It seemed to me if we went down we'd go down cheering. We walked out the front door. When I hit the lawn I called into the megaphone. "Good morning, Rocky Shores!"

45

WE GOT OFF TO A GOOD START.

Vince double-timed it up to the loft. I called for people with logged-in bikes to make a line to the right. They did this so perfectly it made me think of the biking lanes that had formed along the highway in recent days. "Okay, now this is Lil and this is Mattie." They both waved. "They'll fetch your bike for you if it's already here. If you are new today and you know you need brakes or if your bike is hard to pedal, please move to the far left and go to the workbench marked BRAKES." Robert raised his hands and pointed to the sign at his work station. Again, they split up in an orderly way.

I overheard a man say, "I'll wait in any line he tells me to. I took the day off to be here. I figure it's well worth it." He smiled and nodded to a couple of kids who were pushing trail bikes.

I called for Flats next and moved them two steps left. "Officer Runkle will get you started," I called. "You're in good hands. He's had a few flats on the Rocky Shore's bike beat. He knows what he's doing." That made the crowd laugh. I felt my face flush. I couldn't help grinning. Maybe this *was* going to work. I called for Ragged Shifting and Fallen Chains.

So it went.

We had several diagnostic huddles going. People conversing and nodding. Cooperating! Excellent, I thought. Now how am I going to make it around to these other stations? I was the runner. I knew this part would be tough. And more "takers," as Robert had called them, were arriving.

Lil rushed up and said, "Mattie will keep fetching. I'll greet people and send them to the stations. I listened to you, Dewey. I can do it." I handed her the megaphone.

On my way to the Ragged Shifting station, I saw Pop Chilly out of the corner of my eye. He gave me a quick thumbs-up. "Great start, Dewey!" I waved back. He had Angus and Eva involved in something that had to do with a big tin can and a poster and some string. I couldn't stop to find out what he was up to.

I told my Ragged Shifters, "Okay, believe it or not, your problem can be as simple as a sticky link in the chain that makes it *feel like* your shifters aren't working. So let's start there. Then we'll work our way back from the derailleurs to the cables until we meet the problem." People were focused. Willing. This was good. I moved two people over to the Chains bench to try lubricating. Then I ran one guy and his bike up to the Genius Loft to see Vince—his first customer of the day. When I felt like Vince was comfortable talking to the guy, I ran back down the stairs. I strung the rope across, as promised.

It was still a sort of triage, I thought. It was also like putting out fires. Lots and lots of fires. I swung out of the shop and glanced beyond the yard to the driveway. People were still arriving. Then a few flashes of purple and white caught my eye.

Team Bocci?

Sure enough. There were three touring bikes— all loaded down, one with a trailer in tow. One of the riders came toward me, peeling off his helmet. "Hey," he said. "It's Dewey, right? Dewey Marriss?"

I recognized him, and the others, too. They were all members of Mr. Bocci's team. They were also crackerjack mechanics. We shook hands.

"We hoped we could help. Where do you want us?"

"W-want you?" I said dumbly.

"Is it okay if we roll the trailer up here? Will it be in the way?"

"N-no," I said, still being stupid.

"Oh, hey, look," one guy told the others. He pointed to one of my station signs. "He's got it divided up already."

"Oh, perfect," the first guy said. He pulled a portable bike stand from the cargo and started assembling it at one of the stations. "Is this good?" he asked me. "We've got two more. And a truing stand."

"This . . . is *great*," I said. "But you should know . . . uh . . . it's a *free* clinic, really. These people aren't expecting to pay for labor."

"Free." The guy smiled. "Yeah. We saw your sign. We're cool with that. We're volunteers." His team began unpacking the trailer—make that *a treasure chest on wheels*; it was full of parts.

"I-I will make sure you get paid for the parts, though," I said.

"We'll collect as we go. Oh, I almost forgot. Mr. Bocci says hi."

Helpfulness is contagious. Not only did I have Team Bocci on my side, I had a lot of the day's "takers" on my side too. But they were not just takers. They were also *givers*.

"Adjusting a bottom bracket? I can do it!" I heard one woman calling. "I just learned. Did it right here." She waved a cheat sheet over her head and pointed to her bike. "I can help you!"

It happened over and over again all morning long. People stayed to help each other.

Meanwhile, Pop Chilly strung that tin can from a pine branch and stuck a poster on the tree that said WHAT'S TODAY WORTH TO YOU? He found himself a stick and every so often he'd give that can a nice noisy beating just to point it out to everyone.

"Pop," I whispered a reminder. "It's supposed to be a *free* clinic. Don't embarrass anyone if—"

"Baw!" said Pop. "I'm a geezer! Geezers get away with whatever! Ask the expert," he said, and he motioned to the fence, where Mr. Spivey was leaning on his elbows and observing. What could I do? This was not a day that I could stop to steer geezers.

It was past noon before I paused to look around again. The sun was high and bright. The yard was hot. I was exhausted and drenched in sweat. But the clinic was going great. With Team Bocci's help, we had every station manned. Runks was working his way through flats. Lil had joined forces with him—in command of the compressor. Vince was calm and productive in the loft.

Suddenly, my body called on breakfast—the one I had not eaten.

I was starved.

I was also sorry. I had a lot of helpers and they probably all needed food. I was about to pull Lil off the compressor and beg her to go open a bunch of sardines or something when I saw Mattie throw a cloth over our picnic table. She set out a stack of paper plates and napkins.

Then Mrs. Bertalli came riding up on her bike. Her boys followed close behind her, along with two more bikers—a man I did not know and a woman with a toddler on the back of her bike, who I thought looked familiar. They were loaded down with canvas grocery bags.

Food! Somebody had a plan.

"Okay now," Mrs. B called to her sons. "Chris and Carl, bring those sandwiches over here on this end, boys. And Frederick, how about a little shade for your pasta salads?"

"Don't forget, I have ham-and-honey-mustard and beef and Boursin biscuits coming, too."

"They're bringing the chicken wings and cole-slaw, too," said the lady with the baby.

"So make us some room!" Frederick, whoever he was, gave Mrs. Bertalli a friendly nudge and she laughed.

It sounded to me like someone else must be coming. Then I heard it—the electric hum.

The Rocky Shores Police Department's wheelie

pod pulled into our driveway. Mrs. Bertalli and her friends let out a cheer. Smiling and laughing, two officers unloaded a couple of coolers and several boxes.

"Mattie, sweetheart, where's that pitcher for lemonade?" Mrs. B set to slicing lemons. Lil appeared out of nowhere to steal a slice.

I took a break and jogged over. "Mrs. Bertalli! Wow! What's all of this?" I asked.

But it was the man called Frederick who supplied the answer. "Think of this as a few pounds of gratitude with a little bit of mayo."

"Gratitude?" Lil and I looked at each other.

"You kids don't know the half of it. But my deli was robbed three times before you spray-painted the culprit. I didn't even know at first. In fact, that young officer had me so confused. He called me each time to tell me he'd found my door jimmied open. I was so grateful to him. But it never seemed like much was missing. So I put in a security camera, check the tapes, and *who* do I think I see walking away in the middle of the night with a half a rib roast and a six-pound wheel of imported

Fontina cheese on his shoulder?"

"*No!*" Lil said.

"Yessir! And very clever. He took *not so much* each time." Frederick made a pinching gesture with his fingers.

"Yes! That's it!" I nearly exploded. Lil locked eyes with me for just a second and gave me a slight nod.

"But I'm not the only one," Frederick said.

"That's right." The lady with the toddler turned to me. "I don't know if you remember me. You fixed my bike. I own McKinnon's Grill."

"Oh!" I said. "Mrs. McKinnon—Big M, small c, big K . . ."

She laughed and said, "That's right. The thief hit my business, too. Same story. The thing was, none of us could be positive who it was on those murky security tapes. But once you spray-painted him . . . well, you know the rest. We're very grateful. When we saw the signs for the clinic we wanted to be a part of it, and your friend Mrs. Bertalli got us organized."

"So, here's lunch!" Frederick said.

"And we've got something for everybody," Mrs. Bertalli said. "Eat! Eat! You must be famished. Let's get everyone."

"I can do it!" Eva called, and she ran up onto the porch and rang the bell. Suddenly Angus's voice came over the police megaphone.

"Anybody hungry out there?"

So friends, takers, givers, Boccis, and even a neighbor all had lunch together. Pop Chilly called Mr. Spivey over, and he came.

"Here," Pop said. He pushed his can-whacking stick into the Spive's hands. "Drum for your supper. I'm taking a break. You manage the can."

Lil and I looked at each other. We both started laughing so hard I thought pasta salad would come out her nose.

46

AT THE END OF THE DAY VINCE AND I SAT slumped in the open door of the shop. "I can hardly move," I said.

Vince grunted back in agreement. "But it worked," he said. "The clinic was the way to go. People were so *nice*."

"A lot of them came to find me just to say thank you. And Pop said there was a lot of cash in that can. And could you *believe* the Boccis showed up? Saved our tails!"

"And that food . . ." said Vince.

"Hmm. Food. Man, how long ago was lunch? I am ready to chow down again." I straightened my legs and groaned. "Or maybe I'll just crash straight into my pillow."

Vince looked at me. "Let's face it; you'll eat," he said. "By the way, you smell."

"Yeah. You too." I returned the compliment.

"Race you for the first shower?"

"Ugh. If you can run, you go for it. I'm going to take a minute and sweep up. Slowly."

"Sure," he said. He bent one knee, then the other. He rose up with a groan and walked away on tired legs.

The shop looked skeletal. Empty bike stands, bare shelves, the workbench littered with just a few pink order slips. Only a few bikes remained. A couple of them were terminal cases. One, seatless with a drooping chain. Two more stripped down to the frames for parts.

I spoke into the air. "Dad," I said, "we did it."

I ran the Shop-Vac over the place. I pushed together a pile of paper trash—boxes from parts, mostly—into the middle of the floor. When I looked around for the recycling bin, I remembered that Lil had moved it out back by the scaffold. I walked out behind the barn. Mr. Spivey was sitting on his stoop. I gave him a nod. He could say anything, ask for anything right now, and it'd be impossible to sidetrack me. I had a plan: Drag that bin around to the shop and fill it. Wash up. Eat the world's biggest dinner. Fall into bed. The last thing I expected as I rounded the corner was an adrenaline rush. But, boy, did I get one.

There stood Officer Macey—right beside the scaffold. My heart struck my ribs hard. *"Macey,"* I said. I may have only whispered it.

"D-Dewey!" He stared back at me, eyes huge. "I-I didn't expect to see you." His face reddened. He looked strange, worn and scared, and not even so powerful anymore. "L-look, I know I've done a lot of wrong and I'm sor—"

"No!" I bellowed at him. Suddenly I felt as big as a bear. "You're *not* supposed to be here!" I took a step toward him. "You're *never* supposed to be here!" I picked up Lil's paint sprayer. It wasn't even attached to the compressor anymore, but it felt good in my hand. I shook it at Macey. He held his palms out toward me and glanced nervously behind him.

"I know I can't make it all right," he said. "B-but maybe I can fix one small part." He took a few steps backward and motioned for me to follow him around the scaffold. "Let me show you. *Please.*"

I went.

Two very familiar junior bikes were leaned up against the barn at the base of Lil's mural. "Oh, you plug of sludge!" I glared at Macey. "You're just trying to save your hide now! You think I'll forgive you for returning stolen—"

"It wasn't me! I didn't take these! I found them stashed between the Dumpster and the fence at the beach. I knew they had to be yours. They're hand built. Who puts quality components on baby bikes?"

"Oh, I know they're ours," I said.

Macey shook his head. "Like I said, I've done so much wrong. But I worked on recovering these from the start. Honest—"

Something whizzed by my ear. I heard a crack and a splat. Macey jumped and squawked. Eggshells and yellow goo oozed down the front of his shirt. He and I looked at each other—both surprised. I turned to look behind me.

In his yard, Mr. Spivey wound back for another

pitch. Macey tried to duck, but a second egg broke against the bare skin of his neck.

"Hate to waste another on you," the Spive crowed. "But I will if I have to! And I'm a witness!" His finger pecked at the ground. "I'll see you go down."

Macey took a few steps backward. He made the slightest move to turn and go. But suddenly a foul and familiar smell filled the air. There came Sprocket, climbing up over the Spive's junk pile. He stepped onto the fence post and jumped down to the ground like he'd been practicing for the moment. The goat stood between Macey and me.

Macey's eyes opened up wide.

One awesome thing about a billy goat is the way it lowers its head but keeps its eyes on its target. Another is the way it gathers speed over a short distance. Macey braced and took the hit in his thigh. He stumbled against the bikes. Caught a pedal in the ankle and winced. He hopped backward, tripping and trying to untangle himself.

Sprocket rallied on his haunches.

"Oh! Sheesh! Call him off!" Macey begged.

"Yeah, it doesn't really work like that," I said.

I gave my head a scratch. "Not like a dog who will lick your boots for a few biscuits."

Macey gave me a desperate look as Sprocket bowed again.

"You could try running," I said.

"W-w-will he chase me?"

"Don't know," I said. "He's a goat. He thinks in a straight line. But you're fast. You could get lucky."

With that, Macey turned and ran. Sprocket pawed the ground with his hoof and gave up his war with a single snort.

I glanced at the Spive. There was something weird on his face. A smile. "Got your brush cutter back," he said. He pointed to Sprocket with his chin.

"Guess so," I said. I pulled up a few wild carrots from right there by the fence and held them out to the old goat—to Sprocket, that is. I walked him to the gate and flipped the latch. Sprocket walked inside.

I turned to my neighbor. "Thanks for backing me up, Mr. Spivey."

He barely let me finish before he threw his arm forward and pecked at the ground with his finger. "All that paper came down in the storm. Made a terrible mess."

"Paper? You mean the pine tree came down. Yes. We'll take care of it eventuall—"

"Naw, naw, naw! I'm saying *the paper* got wet and it all came down!" Mr. Spivey tucked his chin. Pecked some more. Either he was back to yelling at me again or he was trying to show me something.

I turned and looked at the narrow side yard. I'd been distracted before, but now I saw the big curls of brown and blue paper lying on the grass. I looked up at the wall. Took it in slowly. Lil's mural had unveiled itself, and it was awesome.

It took one loud whistle and I had everyone running to join me—Pop and Mattie, Runks and Robert, Vince, Angus, Eva, and Lil.

"Hey! Hey!" I shouted. I stood the little bikes up. "We've got ourselves a couple of miracles out here!"

Angus and Eva shapes flew everywhere. They swirled in paint patterns on the barn wall above us while the two live models sailed by at ground level on their junior bikes.

"How the heck?" Vince said. "Did the bikes just . . . *appear*?"

I would not speak Macey's name. I whispered, "I'll tell you later." Then I said out loud, "This is just a day when everything went right."

"We made history!" The twins squealed. They rode around the barn, down to the far pasture and back again.

Lil stood looking up at the mural. She made binoculars with her hands against her eyes. She let out a breath. "It's really not finished yet. I want to add some details. I'm thinking I want metal. I want edge. I want shine . . ." She made a fist and held it close to her chest.

47

I THINK IT WAS POP AND ROBERT WHO TEAMED up to make dinner. Leftovers from lunch and a platter of fire-roasted vegetables with cheese and summer sausage rendered me speechless for at least twenty minutes. All around me there was talk of how well the clinic had gone.

"Dewey, that was brilliant," Lil said. She gave me a rough sideways hug that made me slop my milk.

"Nope, nope," I said. I raised a finger and made them wait while I drained my glass. "It worked because of the people. It's crazy. But Dad was right. The people were the answer. I am just glad he won't come home to—"

Timing is everything. The phone rang and

Vince ran for it. He came out of the house. "It's Mom," he said, and handed the phone to Lil.

Lil listened and then said, "You are? You're sure?" Her voice sounded strange. So hesitant, so careful. "Okay. Then we'll be watching."

My sister looked at me when she said, "They're coming home."

Why was it the last thing I expected to hear when it was the very thing we'd all waited for?

Lil held on a minute more, still listening to Mom and nodding slowly. At the end of the call she collapsed onto Mattie's shoulder and started to cry. Mattie closed her arms around Lil.

"What's the matter?" Eva asked. "They're coming! Right?"

"Yes, yes," Mattie said. "It's all good." She gave Lil another squeeze.

"They have a new friend—another trucker." Lil finally choked it out. "He—he's going to leave his own rig and drive them home."

"Awesome," said Vince.

"Good people on the highway," Robert said quietly. "Every day."

"Do we have an ETA?" I asked.

"Sunrise," said Lil. "As long as Dad feels okay to sit upright that long."

I thought about what they'd be coming home to. The main garden was full. There were tomatoes to can and cucumbers to pickle. There was a downed pine tree in the far pasture, and probably a bit too much dirty laundry in the house. But there were *not* too many bikes in the barn, and that'd probably hold true at least until sunrise. Goats were still giving and hens were still laying. I thought that wasn't too bad. Not too bad at all.

I chose a short night of sleep for all of us. I set my alarm for 4:33. Then one hour before sunrise, I tugged all my siblings from their beds.

Still in our nightclothes, we walked out to the driveway together. Angus and Eva trotted ahead of us with two puzzled dogs zigzagging across their path. Vince shook off sleep and jogged to catch up to them. Lil walked next to me.

"Hey, Dew, I've been meaning to say something." Lil spoke quietly. "I didn't give you enough credit," she said.

"For . . ."

"Running that Bike Barn this summer was a huge job. I know that you weren't just *playing* at it out there."

"No, I think that's called *work*." I scratched my head. I laughed.

"Yeah. Well. I might not have understood. At least not at first." She puffed a breath through her lips. "Anyway, you outlasted me."

"Outlasted you?"

"Hmm. I love you guys *so* much. But the crunch went so long—" She shook her head and caught a breath with a little hiccupping sound. "I was *so* done *being the parents*," she said. I think she might have caught a tear on her shoulder then. Hard to be sure in the half-light.

I waited, then said, "You should do what I'm going to do now."

"What are you going to do?"

"I'm going to *quit* for a while," I said.

"Quit the Bike Barn?" She looked at me in surprise.

"Naw, I can't do that. But I'm going to drop

back on that whole *being the embodiment of responsibility* thing," I said. "It gets tiring, you know that?"

"Yes, it does." She sighed, and then she laughed.

Sitting on the rough beside the highway, I tucked Angus under my right wing and Eva under my left. Vince sat on one side, Lil on the other, while the dogs huffed hot dog breath onto the backs of our necks.

The five of us had come out to this patch on many summer nights. We had come for the stars above, and for the fireflies that hovered over the grass.

But on that very early morning we watched the pairs of diamond-bright headlights coming down the highway.

Finally—*finally*—we saw Dad's rig, hauling the sun behind it, and carrying inside it the only thing any of us really wanted.

AFTERWORD

SCHOOL BEGINS IN TWO WEEKS. THEY SAY THERE
will be buses. Angus and Eva are supposed to take
a practice ride before they start kindergarten. Mr.
Spivey gets his weekly egg delivery. But mostly the
twins hang close to Mom, and she hangs close to
them. They've been in the garden. The pantry is
full of new jars of tomatoes.

Vince is still talking about his "What the
Crunch Did for Me" essay. I write my own version
over and over again inside my head. I like thinking about the crunch in the past tense. But I'm not
so sure we're there yet. The pumps flow, but it's
unpredictable. Red flags come and go. Sometimes
it all seems pretty random.

The Bike Barn is still busy. I still work every

day, but the pressure is off of me because Dad is home. He feels pretty well, he says, and he does the best he can with repairs.

The other day he told me, "Look, Dew! Turns out I've got a good elbow on the end of this bad hand." He uses that elbow to pin this or that to the bench while the fingers on his good hand work through a repair.

Robert appreciates Dad's humor. We've kept him on in the shop. We need him. Lil is finally cool with all that, now that it's Dad's decision, and I guess I get that.

Lil's out back again most days, working on her mural. She does a lot of *gazing* and says she feels stuck. But this morning she got a new push. Robert showed up with a gift for her: a cardboard box full of brass tacks and doorknobs, copper scraps, and drawer pulls. Then they sat in the grass together, talking, while Lil examined every piece of the treasure.

I left them to it. I went back to the Bike Barn. I was following an urge. I dug through the spindles and picked a job—one that I really felt like doing. Forget triage. Forget the order of things. I settled on a wheel that needed truing. There's nothing like watching something spin just the way it should.

ACKNOWLEDGMENTS

Wow! What a bike ride!

I have the good fortune to pedal with a pack of *the best* friends, family members, and professional contacts a life could offer. Forgive me for not mentioning every one of you by name (I'm really, really tired), but please know that I am grateful.

Special thanks to:

~Katherine, for your patience and rock-solid faith, even when I was miles behind.

~Jennie, for patching the potholes.

~Teresa, for checking the pace of things.

~Leslie B., Doe, Mary-Kelly, Judy, Nancy Eliz, Nancy A., Lorraine, and Kay, for listening to me spin, for steering me 'round the curves, and for providing a whole lot of grease for this race. (You are tireless wonders.)

~Mary, Paula, Thea, and Debbie, for well-timed swallows of cool water.

~The *irrepressible* Ethel Bacon, for just *being*. (She never feared speed, and she perfected the art of trespassing to the point of being invited back multiple times.) Miss you.

~Nancy and Sandi, for arriving with the first-aid kit that time my bike and I took a wicked skidder in the gravel, for setting me gently back on the pavement, and for being the very wind at my back for all the rest of those miles. (Honestly, if not for you . . .)

~Mom, Dad, Carey, and Denny, for checkpoint activity; Mac, for the music; Jess, for the overnights.

~Mark and Jan, for wise thoughts about the creative process, and for always being there to climb hills with me.

~Shep and Luna (yes, honestly), for your unconditional love and all the goodness and greatness inside of you.

~Jonathan, Sam, Marley, and Ian, for *always* keeping my tires pumped for the lifelong ride we take together; you are champions and heroes.

~Last mention: Nick, your joyful spirit and tinker's heart placed you relentlessly in my thoughts all along this journey. Peace now, beautiful boy.